"One of the best book
surprising. Matilda is
cal island where the l
the only white perso
the tiny school wher
novel *Great Expectati*
age, beauty, memories and sudden violence are the main elements of this extraordinary book." —Isabel Allende

"Lloyd Jones's spare, haunting fable explores the power and limitations of art." —*Washington Post Book World*

"Rarely . . . can any novel have combined charm, horror and uplift in quite such superabundance." —*Independent*

"Jones has created a microcosm of postcolonial literature, hybridising the narratives of black and white races to create a new and resonant fable. . . . *Mister Pip* is the first of Jones's six novels to have travelled from his native New Zealand to the U.K. It is to be hoped that it won't be the last." —*Guardian*

"The power of great literature is at the heart of this affecting tale . . . a brilliantly nuanced examination of the power of imagination, literature and reinvention . . . *Mister Pip* is a powerful and humane novel from one of New Zealand's top writers." —*Financial Times*

"It's clear from the first page that [*Mister Pip*] is prizewinning stuff . . . being a truthful writer, Jones sees nothing—neither his heroes nor his villains in black and white. His is a bold inquiry into the way that we construct and repair our communities, and ourselves, with stories old and new." —*Times* (London)

"*Mister Pip* is a poignant and impressive work which can take its place alongside the classical novels of adolescence."

—*Times Literary Supplement*

"*Mister Pip* is a powerful and touching story about one man's role in transforming the lives of young people. Every high school teacher and student should read this book."

—Erin Gruwell, author of *The Freedom Writers Diary*

"[An] eloquent homage to the power of storytelling . . . The accessible narrative, with its direct and graceful prose, belies the sophistication of its telling as Jones addresses head-on the effects of imperialism and the redemptive power of art."

—*Booklist*

"*Mister Pip* is an assured tribute to the remarkable ability of literature to see us through adversities and tribulations."

—*Milwaukee Journal Sentinel*

"A tribute to the magic of story and the power of teachers."

—*Parade*

OTHER BOOKS BY THE AUTHOR

Swimming to Australia

Biografi

This House Has Three Walls

Choo Woo

The Book of Fame

Here at the End of the World We Learn to Dance

Paint Your Wife

Mister Pip

Lloyd Jones

A DELL BOOK

MISTER PIP
A Dell Book

PUBLISHING HISTORY
First published by The Text Publishing Company, Australia, 2006
Dial Press hardcover edition / August 2007
Dell international mass market edition / February 2008

Published by
Bantam Dell
A Division of Random House, Inc.
New York, New York

This is a work of fiction. Names, characters, places, and incidents either are the product of the author's imagination or are used fictitiously. Any resemblance to actual persons, living or dead, events, or locales is entirely coincidental.

Cover design by Roberto de Vicq de Cumptich
Cover photograph by Jo McRyan, Getty Images

Book design by Virginia Norey

Library of Congress Catalog Card Number: 2007005224

ISBN 978-0-440-29685-0

Printed in the United States of America
Published simultaneously in Canada

www.bantamdell.com

OPM 10 9 8 7 6 5 4 3 2 1

To my family

“Characters migrate.”

—*Umberto Eco*

EVERYONE CALLED HIM POP EYE. EVEN IN those days, when I was a skinny thirteen-year-old, I thought he probably knew about his nickname but didn't care. His eyes were too interested in what lay up ahead to notice us barefoot kids.

He looked like someone who had seen or known great suffering and hadn't been able to forget it. His large eyes in his large head stuck out further than anyone else's—like they wanted to leave the surface of his face. They made you think of someone who can't get out of the house quickly enough.

Pop Eye wore the same white linen suit every day. His trousers snagged on his bony knees in the sloppy heat. Some days he wore a clown's nose. His nose was already big. He didn't need that red lightbulb. But for reasons we couldn't think of he wore the red nose on certain days—which may have meant something to him. We never saw him smile. And on those days he wore the clown's nose you found yourself looking away because you never saw such sadness.

He pulled a piece of rope attached to a trolley on which Mrs. Pop Eye stood. She looked like an ice queen. Nearly every woman on our island had crinkled hair, but Grace had straightened hers. She wore it piled up, and in the absence of a crown her hair did the trick. She looked so proud, as if she had no idea of her own bare feet. You saw her huge bum and worried about the toilet seat. You thought of her mother and birth and that stuff.

At two-thirty in the afternoon the parrots sat in the shade of the trees and looked down at a human shadow one-third longer than any seen before. There were only the two of them, Mr. and Mrs. Pop Eye, yet it felt like a procession.

The younger kids saw an opportunity and so fell in behind. Our parents looked away. They would rather stare at a colony of ants moving over a rotting pawpaw. Some stood by with their idle machetes, waiting for the spectacle to pass. For the younger kids the sight consisted only of a white man towing a black woman. They saw what the parrots saw, and what the dogs saw while sitting on their scrawny arses snapping their jaws at a passing mosquito. Us older kids sensed a bigger story. Sometimes we caught a snatch of conversation. Mrs. Watts was as mad as a goose. Mr. Watts was doing penance for an old crime. Or maybe it was the result of a bet. The sight represented a bit of uncertainty in our world, which in every other way knew only sameness.

Mrs. Pop Eye held a blue parasol to shade herself from the sun. It was the only parasol in the whole of the island, so we heard. We didn't ask after all the black umbrellas we saw, let alone the question: what was the difference between these black umbrellas and the parasol? And not because we cared if we looked dumb, but because if you went too far with a question like that one, it could turn a rare thing into a commonplace thing. We loved that word—*parasol*—and we weren't about to lose it just because of some dumb-arse question. Also, we knew, whoever asked that question would get a hiding, and serve them bloody right too.

They didn't have any kids. Or if they did they were grown up and living somewhere else, maybe in America, or Australia or Great Britain. They had names. She was Grace and black like us. He was Tom Christian Watts and white as the whites of your eyes, only sicker.

There are some English names on the headstones in the church graveyard. The doctor on the other side of the island had a full Anglo-Saxon name even though he was black like the rest of us. So, although we knew him as Pop Eye we used to say "Mr. Watts" because it was the only name like it left in our district.

They lived alone in the minister's old house. You couldn't see it from the road. It used to be surrounded by grass, according to my mum. But after the minister died the authorities forgot about the mission and the lawn mower rusted. Soon the bush grew up around the house, and by the time I was born Mr. and Mrs. Pop Eye had sunk out of view of the world. The only times we saw them was when Pop Eye, looking like a tired old nag circling the well, pulled his wife along in the trolley. The trolley had bamboo rails. Mrs. Pop Eye rested her hands on these.

To be a show-off you need an audience. But Mrs. Pop Eye didn't pay us any attention. We weren't worthy of that. It was as if we didn't exist. Not that we cared. Mr. Watts interested us more.

Because Pop Eye was the only white for miles around, little kids stared at him until their ice blocks melted over their black hands. Older kids sucked in their breath and knocked on his door to ask to do their "school project" on him. When the door opened some just froze and stared. I knew an older girl who was invited in; not everyone was. She said there were books everywhere. She asked him to talk about his life. She sat in a chair next to a glass of water he had poured for her, pencil in hand, notebook open. He said: "My dear, there has been a great deal of it. I expect more of the same." She wrote this down. She showed her teacher, who praised her initiative. She even brought it over to our house to show me and my mum, which is how I know about it.

It wasn't just for the fact he was the last white man that made Pop Eye what he was to us—a source of mystery mainly, but also confirmation of something else we held to be true.

We had grown up believing white to be the color of all the important things, like ice cream, aspirin, ribbon, the moon, the stars. White stars and a full moon were more important when my grandfather grew up than they are now that we have generators.

When our ancestors saw the first white they thought they were looking at ghosts or maybe some people who had just fallen into bad luck. Dogs sat on their tails and opened their jaws to await the spectacle. The dogs thought they were in for a treat. Maybe these white people could jump backwards or somersault over trees. Maybe they had some spare food. Dogs always hope for that.

The first white my grandfather saw was a shipwrecked yachtsman who asked him for a compass. My grandfather didn't know what a compass was, so he knew he didn't have one. I picture him clasping his hands at his back and smiling. He wouldn't want to appear dumb. The white man asked for a map. My grandfather didn't know what he was asking for, and so pointed down at the man's cut feet. My grandfather wondered how the sharks had missed that bait. The white man asked where he had washed up. At last my grandfather could help. He said it was an island. The white man asked if the island had a name. My grandfather replied with the word that means "island." When the man asked directions to the nearest shop, my grandfather burst out laughing. He pointed up at a coconut tree and back over the white's shoulder whence he had come, meaning the bloody great ocean stocked with fish. I have always liked that story.

Other than Pop Eye or Mr. Watts, and some Australian mine workers, I'd seen few other living whites. The ones I had seen were in an old film. At school we were shown the visit by the duke of something or other many years before in nineteen-hundred-and-something. The camera kept staring at the duke and saying nothing. We watched the duke eat. The duke and the other whites wore mustaches and white trousers. They even wore buttoned-up jackets. They weren't any good at sitting on the ground either. They kept rolling over onto their elbows. We all laughed—us kids—at the whites trying to sit on the ground as they would in a chair. They were handed pig trotters in banana leaves. One man in a helmet could be seen asking for something. We didn't know what until he was brought a piece of white cloth, which he used to wipe his mouth. We roared our heads off laughing.

Mostly, though, I was watching out for my grandfather. He was one of the skinny kids marching by in bare feet and white singlets. My grandfather was the second to top kid kneeling in a human pyramid in front of the white men in helmets eating pig trotters. Our class was asked to write an essay on what we had seen, but I had no idea what it was about. I didn't understand the meaning of it so I wrote about my grandfather and the story he told of the shipwrecked white man he had found washed up like a starfish on the beach of his village, which in those days had no electricity or running water and didn't know Moscow from rum.

WHAT I AM ABOUT TO TELL RESULTS, I think, from our ignorance of the outside world. My mum knew only what the last minister had told her in sermons and conversations. She knew her times tables and the names of some distant capitals. She had heard that man had been to the moon but was inclined not to believe such stories. She did not like boastfulness. She liked even less the thought that she might have been caught out, or made a fool of. She had never left Bougainville. On my eighth birthday I remember thinking to ask her how old she was. She quickly turned her face away from me, and for the first time in my life I realized I had embarrassed her.

Her comeback was a question of her own. "How old do you think I am?"

When I was eleven, my father flew off on a mining plane. Before that, though, he was invited to sit in a classroom and watch films about the country he was going to. There were films on pouring tea: the milk went in the cup first—though when you prepared your bowl of cornflakes the milk went in after. My mum says she and my father argued like roosters over that last one.

Sometimes when I saw her sad I knew she would be thinking back to that argument. She would look up from whatever she was doing to say, "Perhaps I should have shut up. I was too strong. What do you think, girl?" This was one of the few times she was seriously interested in my opinion and, like the question concerning her age, I always knew what to say to cheer her up.

My father was shown other films. He saw cars, trucks, planes. He saw motorways and became excited. But then there was a demonstration of a pedestrian crossing. You had to wait for a boy in a white coat to raise his sign with "sticks up!"

My father got scratchy. There were too many roads with hard edges and these kids in white coats had the power to control traffic with their stop signs. Now they argued again. My mum said it was no different here. You couldn't just walk where you liked. There was a clip over the ear if you strayed. 'Cause, she said, it was as the Good Book says. You might know about heaven but it didn't mean you had entry as of right.

For a while we treasured a postcard my father sent from Townsville. This is what he had to say: Up to the moment the plane entered the clouds he looked down and saw where we lived for the very first time. From out at sea the view is of a series of mountain peaks. From the air he was amazed to see our island look no bigger than a cow pat. But my mum didn't care about that stuff. All my mum wanted to know was if where he had gone to there were pay packets.

A month later there was a second postcard. He said pay packets hung off factory rafters like breadfruit. And that settled it. We were going to join him—that's what we were going to do, when Francis Ona and his rebels declared war on the copper mine and the company, which, in some way that I didn't understand at the time, brought the redskin soldiers from Port Moresby to our island. According to Port Moresby we are one country. According to us we are black as the night. The soldiers looked like people leached up out of the red earth. That's why they were known as redskins.

News of war arrives as bits of maybe and hearsay. Rumor is its mistress. Rumor, which you can choose to believe or ignore. We heard that no one could get in or out. We didn't know what to make of that, because how could you seal off a country? What would you tie it up in or wrap around it? We didn't know what to believe, then the redskin soldiers arrived, and we learned about the blockade.

We were surrounded by sea, and while the redskins' gunboats patrolled the coastline their helicopters flew overhead. There was no newspaper or radio to guide our thoughts. We relied on word of mouth. The redskins were going to choke the island and the rebels into submission. That's what we heard. "Good luck to them," said my mum. That's how much we cared. We had fish. We had our chickens. We had our fruits. We had what we had always had. In addition to that, a rebel supporter could add, "We had our pride."

Then, one night, the lights went out for good. There was no more fuel for the generators. We heard the rebels had broken into the hospital in Arawa, further down the coast, and taken all the medical supplies. That news really worried our mums, and soon the littlest kids came down with malaria and there was nothing that could be done to help them. We buried them and dragged their weeping mothers away from their tiny graves.

Us kids hung around with our mums. We helped in the gardens. We stalked each other beneath trees that rise several hundred feet in the air. We played in the streams that tumble and spill down steep hillsides. We found new pools in which to look for our floating faces of mischief. We played in the sea and our black skins got blacker under the sun.

We stopped going to school after our teachers had left on the last boat for Rabaul. *The last boat.* That sentence made our faces droop. We'd have to walk on water to get off the island now.

Everyone was surprised that Pop Eye didn't leave when he had the chance. Even though Mrs. Watts was a local he could have taken her. The other whites did. They took their wives and girlfriends. These were company men, of course. No one knew what Pop Eye did; he did no work as far as we could tell. He was invisible for most of the time.

Our houses sat beached in a sloppy row, all of them gaping back at the sea. Doors and windows were always left open, so it was easy to overhear the conversation of neighbors. Nobody heard the conversation of the Wattses because of the distance between our thirty or so houses and the old mission house where they lived.

Sometimes you saw Mr. Watts at one end of the beach or caught a glimpse of his back, and then you wondered where he had been and what he had been doing. And there were those strange processions. The Wattses would come into view near the classroom block. As they arrived at the first houses chickens and roosters wandered out to meet them. At the end of the row Mr. Watts towed his wife across the lumpy grass and past the pigpens to the bush line. We sat in the trees, waiting for them to pass beneath our dangling feet. We hoped he might stop for a break and a word with Mrs. Watts, because no one had seen them speaking together as man and wife. In any case, to catch Mrs. Watts' ear you felt the language would have to be big, even enormous, scripted out in a series of lightning bolts.

It was easy to accept she was mad. Mr. Watts was more of a mystery because he'd come out of a world we didn't really know. My mum said his tribe had forgotten him. They wouldn't have left behind a company man.

I did not realize what a big impact the school had on my

life until it closed. My sense of time was governed by the school year—when term began, when it ended, the holidays between. Now that we had been set free we had all this time on our hands. When we woke we no longer felt the brooms on our backsides or our mums shouting at us to *Ged up! Ged up, you lazybones!*

We still woke when the roosters did, but now we lay there, listening to the dogs open their jaws and growl in their sleep. We also listened out for the mosquito, which we feared more than the redskins or the rebels.

We learned to eavesdrop on our parents—though some things we could see for ourselves. We were used to the redskins' helicopters buzzing in and out of the cloud around the mountain peaks. Now we saw them head out to sea in a straight line. The helicopter would reach a certain point, then turn around and come back as if it had forgotten something. Where they turned back was just a pinprick in the distance. We could not see the men thrown out. But that's what we heard. The redskins flung the captured rebels out the open door of the helicopter, their arms and legs kicking in the air. And whenever us kids strayed into range our mums and dads would stop talking, and so we knew, didn't we, that there was some fresh atrocity, the details we didn't yet know about.

The weeks passed. Now we had an idea of what our time was for. It was to be spent waiting. We waited, and we waited for the redskin soldiers, or the rebels, whoever got here first. It was a long, long time before they came to our village. But I know exactly when they did because that's what I had made up my mind to do—I had decided I would keep the time. It was three days before my fourteenth birthday when the redskins came into our village for the first time. Four weeks later the rebels arrived. But in the time leading up to those calamitous events, Pop Eye and his wife, Grace, came back into our lives.

GED UP, MATILDA," MY MUM YELLED ONE morning. "You've got school today." She must have enjoyed that moment. I could tell it cheered her up just to say it. As if we had slipped back into a comfortable old routine. I happened to know it was a Wednesday. My mum wouldn't have known that. I kept a pencil under my mat. And a calendar of days on the corner post.

My mum swept her broom near my head. She shouted at a rooster that had flown in the door.

"But we have no teachers," I said.

And with a glimmer of a smile, my mum said, "You do now. Pop Eye is going to teach you kids."

*

BOUGAINVILLE IS ONE of the most fertile places on earth. Drop a seed in the soil and three months later it is a plant with shiny green leaves. Another three months and you are picking its fruit. But for a machete, we would have no land of our own. Left alone the bush would march down the steep hillsides and bury our villages in flower and vine.

This is why it was easy to forget there had ever been a school. Creepers had smothered two trees in purple and red flowers, as if to soften the blow, and by that way crept onto the school roof; they had climbed in the windows and found a way across the ceiling. Another six months and our school would have disappeared from view.

We were all ages, from seven to fifteen. I counted twenty kids, about half the original school roll. I knew of two older boys who had gone off into the mountains to join the rebels. Three other families had left on that last boat to Rabaul. I don't know about the rest. Maybe they hadn't heard about the school opening. Over the coming weeks a few boys would return.

Pop Eye was waiting for us inside. It was almost dark, though light enough to make out the tall thin white man in his linen suit. He stood at the front of the class, his eyes glancing away from our inspection. Everyone looked to see if he was wearing his red clown's nose. He wasn't. But there were other changes since I last saw him. His hair was long, nearly touching his shoulders. When it was short we hadn't noticed the flecks of red and gray. His beard spilled down onto his chest.

Our last teacher had been Mrs. Siau. She was a small woman, not much bigger than us younger kids. Pop Eye stood where she had and so he seemed too large for the room. His white hands relaxed at his sides. He didn't look to where we were filing in the door. His eyes were fixed on the far end of the classroom. They didn't budge—not even when a black dog came in wagging his tail. That was encouraging, because Mrs. Siau would have clapped her hands and aimed a foot at that dog's arse.

This was school, but not how I remembered it. Perhaps that's why everything felt strange, as if we were trying to squeeze into an old life that didn't exist anymore, at least not in the way we remembered. We found our old desks and even they felt changed. The cool touch of smooth wood on the backs of my legs was the only thing that was familiar. None of the kids looked at each other. Instead, we stared at our new and unexpected teacher. He seemed to be giving us permission to do exactly that. When the last of us took our places Pop Eye snapped out of his trance.

He looked at our faces, taking each of us in, though careful not to linger. Just noting who had turned up. He signaled with a nod when that job was done. Then he glanced at a green vine hanging down from the ceiling. He reached up for it, tore it down, and bunched it in his hands like it was paper.

I had never heard him speak. As far as I knew, no one in that class had. I don't know what I was expecting, except when he spoke his voice was surprisingly small. He was a big man, and if he had shouted like our mums did he would have brought the roof down. Instead he spoke as if he was addressing each one of us personally.

"I want this to be a place of light," he said. "No matter what happens." He paused there for us to digest this.

When our parents spoke of the future we were given to understand it was an improvement on what we knew. For the first time we were hearing that the future was uncertain. And because this had come from someone outside of our lives we were more ready to listen. He looked around at our faces. If he was expecting a challenge he didn't get one.

"We must clear the space and make it ready for learning," he said. "Make it new again."

When his large eyes rolled away to the open window with its screen of green, that's when I noticed his tie. It was skinny, black, formal, but he'd left the top button of his shirt undone for his body to breathe. He brought up a delicate white hand to touch the knot. Then he turned back to us kids and raised an eyebrow.

"Yes?" he asked.

We looked around at each other and nodded. Someone thought to say "Yes, Mr. Watts," and we all followed suit: "Yes, Mr. Watts."

That's when he held up a finger as though something important had just come to him.

"I know some of you call me Pop Eye. That's okay too. I like Pop Eye."

And for the first time in all the years I'd seen him dragging Mrs. Pop Eye behind in that trolley, he smiled. After that I never called him Pop Eye again.

We set to work. We dragged the flowering vine down off the roof, which was easy enough; it seemed to know what would eventually happen to it, which is why it didn't hold on too tight. We hauled it away from the building to a clearing where we burned it in a thick white smoke. Mr. Watts sent a number of us kids off to find brooms. We swept out the classroom. Later in the day the sun dropped and exposed the cobwebs. We leaped at those with our hands.

We were enjoying our first day back at school. Mr. Watts kept an eye on us. He allowed high spirits. But when he spoke we shut up.

Now we returned to our desks to wait for him to dismiss us and send us home. He spoke in that same quiet voice that had come as such a surprise at the start of the day.

"I want you to understand something. I am no teacher, but I will do my best. That's my promise to you children. I believe, with your parents' help, we can make a difference to our lives."

He stopped there like he'd just had a new thought, and he must have, because next he asked us to get up from our desks and to form a circle. He told us to hold hands or link arms, whatever we saw fit to do.

Some of us who had heard a minister speak and knew about church closed their eyes and dropped their chins onto their chests. But there was no prayer. There was no sermon. Instead, Mr. Watts thanked us all for turning up.

"I wasn't sure you would," he said. "I will be honest with you. I have no wisdom, none at all. The truest thing I can tell you is that whatever we have between us is all we've got. Oh, and of course Mr. Dickens."

Who was Mr. Dickens? And why, in a village population of less than sixty, had we not met him before? Some of the older kids tried to pretend they knew who he was. One even said he was a friend of his uncle's, and encouraged by our interest went on to say he had met Mr. Dickens. His claim was soon exposed by our questions and he sloped off like a kicked dog. It turned out no one knew Mr. Dickens.

"Tomorrow," I told my mum, "we meet Mr. Dickens."

She stopped sweeping and thought. "That's a white man's name." She shook her head and spat out the door. "No. You heard wrong, Matilda. Pop Eye is the last white man. There is no other."

"Mr. Watts says there is."

I had heard Mr. Watts speak. I had heard him say he would always be honest with us kids. If he said we were to meet Mr. Dickens, then I felt sure that we would. I was looking forward to seeing another white man. It never occurred to me to ask where this Mr. Dickens had been hiding himself. But then I had no reason to doubt Mr. Watts' word.

My mum must have reconsidered overnight, because next morning when I ran off to school she called me back.

"This Mr. Dickens, Matilda—if you get the chance, why don't you ask him to fix our generator."

Every other kid turned up to school with similar instructions. They were to ask Mr. Dickens for anti-malaria tablets, aspirin, generator fuel, beer, kerosene, wax candles. We sat at our desks with our shopping lists and waited for Mr. Watts to introduce Mr. Dickens. He wasn't there when we arrived. There was just Mr. Watts, as we had found him the day before, standing tall at the front of the class, lost in a dream, I'd say, because there was nothing left to discover about that back wall. We kept our eyes on the window. We didn't want to miss a white man strolling past.

We could see the beach palms spreading up to a blue sky. And a turquoise sea so still we hardly noticed it. Halfway to the horizon we could see a redskins' gunboat. It was like a gray sea mouse—it crawled along with its guns aimed at us. In the direction of the hills we heard sporadic gunfire. We were used to that sound—sometimes it was the rebels testing their restored rifles—and besides, we knew it was a longer way off than what it sounded. We had come to know the amplifying effects of water, so the gunfire just merged with the background chorus of the grunting pigs and shrieking birds.

While we waited for Mr. Watts to wake from his dream I counted three lime-green geckos and a pale one on the ceiling. A flower-pecker bird flew in the open window and out again. That got our attention because if we had been ready with a net we could have eaten it. As the bird flew out the window, Mr. Watts began to read to us.

I had never been read to in English before. Nor had the others. We didn't have books in our homes, and before the blockade our only books had come from Moresby, and those were written in pidgin. When Mr. Watts read to us we fell quiet. It was a new sound in the world. He read slowly so we heard the shape of each word.

"'My father's family name being Pirrip, and my

Christian name Philip, my infant tongue could make of both names nothing longer or more explicit than Pip. So I called myself Pip, and came to be called Pip.' "

There had been no warning from Mr. Watts. He just began to read. My desk was in the second row from the back. Gilbert Masoi sat in front, and I couldn't see past his fat shoulders and big woolly head. So when I heard Mr. Watts speak I thought he was talking about himself. That he was Pip. It was only as he began to walk between our desks that I saw the book in his hand.

He kept reading and we kept listening. It was some time before he stopped, but when he looked up we sat stunned by the silence. The flow of words had ended. Slowly we stirred back into our bodies and our lives.

Mr. Watts closed the book and held the paperback up in one hand, like a church minister. We saw him smile from one corner of the room to the other. "That was chapter one of *Great Expectations,* which, incidentally, is the greatest novel by the greatest English writer of the nineteenth century, Charles Dickens."

Now we felt silly as bats for thinking we were going to be introduced to someone by the name of Mr. Dickens. Perhaps Mr. Watts had an idea of what was going on in our heads, though. "When you read the work of a great writer," he told us, "you are making the acquaintance of that person. So you can say you have met Mr. Dickens on the page, so to speak. But you don't know him yet."

One of the younger kids, Mabel, put up her hand to ask a question. At first we thought Mr. Watts hadn't seen her because he carried on over the top of Mabel's waving hand. "I welcome questions. I won't always be able to answer them. Remember that," he said. "Also, when you raise your hand to ask me something, would you be so kind as to give your name."

He nodded in Mabel's direction. She mustn't have taken in what Mr. Watts had just said, because she started to ask her question until Mr. Watts stopped her mid-sentence with a raised eyebrow, which, for the first time in twenty-four hours, reminded us of his nickname.

"Mabel, Mr. Watts," she said.

"Good. I'm very pleased to meet you, Mabel. That is a pretty name," he said.

Mabel shone. She wriggled in her desk. Then she spoke.

"When can we say we know Mr. Dickens?"

Mr. Watts brought two fingers up to his chin. We watched him think for a moment.

"That is a very good question, Mabel. In fact, my first response is that you have asked me something to which there is no answer. But I will give it my best shot. Some of you will know Mr. Dickens when we finish the book. The book is fifty-nine chapters long. If I read a chapter a day, that's fifty-nine days."

This was difficult information to bring home. We had met Mr. Dickens but we did not know him yet, and would not know him for another fifty-eight days. It was December 10, 1991. I quickly calculated—we would not know Mr. Dickens until February 6, 1992.

IN THE TROPICS NIGHT FALLS QUICKLY. There is no lingering memory of the day just been. One moment you can see the dogs looking skinny and mangy. In the next they have turned into black shadows. If you are not ready with candles and kerosene lamps, the quick fall of night is like being put away in a dark cell, from where there is no release until the following dawn.

During the blockade we could not waste fuel or candles. But as the rebels and redskins went on butchering one another, we had another reason for hiding under the cover of night. Mr. Watts had given us kids another world to spend the night in. We could escape to another place. It didn't matter that it was Victorian England. We found we could easily get there. It was just the blimmin' dogs and the blimmin' roosters that tried to keep us here.

By the time Mr. Watts reached the end of chapter one I felt like I had been spoken to by this boy Pip. This boy who I couldn't see to touch but knew by ear. I had found a new friend.

The surprising thing is where I'd found him—not up a

tree or sulking in the shade, or splashing around in one of the hill streams, but in a book. No one had told us kids to look there for a friend. Or that you could slip inside the skin of another. Or travel to another place with marshes, and where, to our ears, the bad people spoke like pirates. I think Mr. Watts enjoyed the spoken parts. When he spoke them he became the voices. That's another thing that impressed us—for the time he was reading, Mr. Watts had a way of absenting himself. And we forgot all about him being there. When Magwitch, the escaped convict, threatens to rip out Pip's heart and liver if he doesn't bring him some food, and a file for his leg irons, we didn't hear Mr. Watts, we heard Magwitch, and it was like the convict was in the classroom with us. We had only to close our eyes to be sure.

There was also a lot of stuff I didn't understand. At night I lay on my mat wondering what marshes were; and what were wittles and leg irons? I had an idea from their sound. *Marshes*. I wondered if quicksand was the same. I knew about quicksand because a man up at the mine had sunk into it, never to be seen again. That happened years earlier when the mine was still open and there were white people crawling over Panguna like ants over a corpse.

Mr. Watts had given us kids another piece of the world. I found I could go back to it as often as I liked. What's more, I could pick up any moment in the story. Not that I thought of what we were hearing as story. No. I was hearing someone give an account of themselves and all that had happened. I was still discovering my favorite bits. Pip in the graveyard surrounded by the headstones of his dead parents and five dead brothers ranked high. We knew about death—we had seen all those babies buried up on the hillside. Me and Pip had something else in common; I was eleven when my father left, so neither of us really knew our fathers.

I'd met mine, of course, but then I only knew my dad as a child knows a parent, as a sort of crude outline filled in with one or two colors. I'd never seen my father scared or cry. I'd never heard him admit to any wrongdoing. I have no idea what he dreamed of. And once I'd seen a smile pinned to one cheek and darkness to the other when my mum had yelled at him. Now he was gone, and I was left with just an impression—one of male warmth, big arms, and loud laughter.

The shape of the letters on the headstone gave Pip the idea his father was a "square, stout, dark man with curly black hair."

Encouraged by Pip's example I tried to build a picture of my own dad. I found some examples of his handwriting. He wrote in small capital letters. What did that say about him? He wanted to be noticed, but not too noticeable? There was that booming laugh of his, of course. I slept in the same room as my mum, and that night in the dark I asked her if Dad was a happy man. She said, "Never at the right time, though usually after he had been drinking."

I asked her if she thought he was a "stout man." In the dark I heard her raise herself up on an elbow. "*Stout!* Where did you get that word from, girl?"

"Mr. Watts."

"Pop Eye. Him," she said as she let herself down again.

"It was in a book."

"What blimmin' book?"

"Great Expectations."

I had given her three quick answers. The last one was the most stunning. I had lost her. I could hear her brooding next to me. She shifted on her mat. I could hear her angry breath. I don't know what made her so angry all the time. As we lay there the night filled up with noise. We listened to the dogs growling at shadows, and to the ocean shuffle up the beach and draw out. We lay like that for a very long time before my mum spoke.

"So, Matilda, aren't you going to tell me about that book?"

This was the first time I had been in a position to tell her anything about the world. But this was a place she did not know about and hadn't heard of. She couldn't even pretend to know, so it was up to me to color in that world for her. I couldn't remember the exact words Mr. Watts had read to us, and I didn't think I would be able to make it possible for my mum to slip into that world that us kids had or into Pip's life or some other's, that of the convict, say. So I told her in my own words about Pip having no mum or dad or brothers, and my mum cried out, "He is lost."

"No," I said. "There is a sister. She is married to a man called Joe. They are the ones who bring up Pip."

I told her about the convict creeping up on Pip in the cemetery. How he threatened to rip out his heart and liver if Pip didn't do what he asked. I told her how Pip went back to the house for a file and food to take to the convict in the morning.

I hadn't done it justice in my telling. There was no sound to what I said. Just the bare facts. And when I reached the end I had to say, "That's all I know, so far."

A dog howled at the night. Something squawked. We heard a high voice from one of the nearby houses. Then my mum spoke.

"What would you do, girl? If a man was hiding in the jungle and he ask you to steal from me. Would you do that?"

"No," I said, and I thanked the Lord for the dark so that my lying face could not be seen.

"Pop Eye should be teaching you kids proper behavior," she said. "I want to know everything that happens in that book. You hear me, Matilda?"

*

WHEN WE WEREN'T being read *Great Expectations* we did our schoolwork, our spelling, our times tables. Mr. Watts got us to memorize countries beginning with A—America, Andorra, Australia—through to Z—Zambia, Zimbabwe. We had no books. We had our minds and we had our memories, and according to Mr. Watts, that's all we needed.

There were gaps in Mr. Watts' knowledge. Large gaps, as it turned out, for which he apologized. He knew the word *chemistry* but could not tell us much more than that.

He handed on the names of famous people such as Darwin, Einstein, Plato, Archimedes, Aristotle. We wondered if he was making them up, because he struggled to explain why they were famous or why we had to know them. Yet he was our teacher and he never relinquished that status. When an unfamiliar fish washed up on the beach it felt right to ask Mr. Watts to come and identify the strange eel-like serpent. It didn't matter that he would end up standing over the creature with the same blank face as the rest of us.

When it came to Mr. Dickens, though, he knew he was on safe ground. And we felt happy for him. He always referred to him as Mr. Dickens—never Dickens or Charles. So we knew what to do when it was our turn to refer to the author. We spoke about Mr. Dickens until he began to feel real, or as real as Mr. Watts. We just didn't know him yet.

Mr. Watts spoke to us about England. He had been there. He might as well have said "the moon." We struggled to think of a question to ask. My friend Celia asked if there were black people there. Mr. Watts answered quickly, "Yes," and as he shifted his attention around the room to look for another, better question, Celia snuck a sideways look at me from under her black pigtails.

We soon learned there were many Englands, and Mr. Watts had only been to two or three of them. The England he visited was very different from the one Mr. Dickens had lived and worked in. This was a challenging notion for those of us who had never been anywhere, because we had the feeling that life on the island was much the same as it had been for our grandfathers and their grandfathers, especially after the blockade was imposed.

My mum liked to tell a story about my grandfather back when he took the steamboat to Rabaul for the first time. He had to nudge another passenger standing up on deck to ask, "What are those large pigs I can see moving behind the trees?" He had just seen his first motorcar.

Away from Mr. Dickens and England, Mr. Watts was lost. Once when Gilbert stuck up his hand to ask how the motorcar worked, Mr. Watts stammered out a reply. He scratched his head. He started again. We all knew about petrol and the key in the ignition. It was the rest of it Gilbert wanted to know about. We were told it was complicated. Mr. Watts said it was easier to explain with a drawing. Once again we were asked to be patient and he would see what he could do.

We knew Mr. Watts was aware of his shortcomings—no one had to tell him—because not long after we resumed school he invited our mums to come into the classroom and share what they knew of the world.

MABEL'S MUM WAS THE FIRST TO COME and speak to us. Mrs. Kabui arrived at the open door in a blaze of late afternoon light. Mr. Watts held out a welcoming hand, and Mrs. Kabui walked quickly towards it. She spoke in a whisper to Mr. Watts. I saw Mabel shift to the edge of her chair. Mr. Watts gave a nod and Mrs. Kabui looked relieved.

"Class, we are very lucky today," began Mr. Watts. "Mrs. Kabui has agreed to share with us the remarkable life and times of the heart seed."

Mabel's mum gave a shy smile. She stood barefoot in a white blouse and a red skirt. As soon as she smiled you forgot the tear in the shoulder of her blouse and the pawing marks left by the grubby fingers of a child. She spoke softly and chose her words with great care.

"Thank you, Mr. Watts. Thank you very much. I am here today hoping to surprise you kids." She looked around to see if we were ready. We were.

"What if I was to tell you that some gardens begin their

lives in oceans?" Again she looked around the class, her gaze skipping over the desk where her daughter sat. Her smile was for us all. "I am here today to talk about the heart seed."

She told us that one day a heart seed floats on the water. The next day it washes up on the beach. The next week the sea breeze and sun have dried it to something light as a husk. The next month sees a wind turn it over and over until it reaches soil. Three months later a sapling grows out of the earth. Nine months later its white flowers open and glance back at the sea whence it came.

"Why am I telling you this, children? Because its stamen makes a fierce flame and keeps away the mosquitoes."

Mr. Watts blinked, like someone just waking up. I have an idea he had been expecting to hear more and that Mabel's mum caught him off-guard with her abrupt ending.

"Very good, Mrs. Kabui. Excellent. The heart seed."

He nodded in our direction, which was a sign for us all to rise and applaud. Mabel clapped her hands the loudest and for the longest. Her mother bent at the hips and dropped her head. She came up laughing. Everyone was pleased. No one had suffered embarrassment or shame.

Great Expectations was next. We knew that. We followed Mr. Watts with our eyes. We watched him pick the book up from his desk. Mabel's mum saw it too. She whispered something to Mr. Watts behind her hand. We heard him say, "Yes, of course. Of course." We saw him gesture to an empty desk and Mabel's mum sat down to be read to from the greatest novel by the greatest English writer of the nineteenth century.

Over and above my own enjoyment I had to listen very carefully because later that night my mum would want an update on Pip. I paid special attention to Mr. Watts' pronunciation. I liked to surprise my mum with a new word she didn't know. What I didn't know at the time was all of us kids were carrying installments of *Great Expectations* back to our families.

The voice that reached me in the dark sounded put out and offended.

"So he took his mother's pork pie."

Pork pie. I grinned in the dark. She didn't know how to say it like Mr. Watts did.

But now I saw I had some explaining to do. The deaths of Pip's mum and dad clearly hadn't sunk in. I'd explained this before, and now I did so all over again. I told her Pip's sister and a man called Joe bring him up—"by hand," I added, having thought about those words and their meaning.

"So he took his sister's pork pie."

"Yes," I conceded.

"And what did Pop Eye have to say about this?"

Mr. Watts hadn't said anything, but I knew this would be the wrong answer.

"Mr. Watts said it is best to wait until all the facts are known."

To this day it impresses me that I was able to come up with that reply. I'm sure I was just repeating what I'd overheard somewhere else, but whenever that was has passed from memory.

I heard my mum shift on her mat. She was waiting for me to go on, but I was equally determined to wait for her to say "Then what happened?"—which she did a few moments later, dragging the words out of herself, irritated at having to ask me.

A rimy morning was the phrase I decided to bring home with me. I used it now to create the picture of Pip carrying the pork pie and file off to the convict Magwitch waiting in the marshes. "It was a rimy morning..."

I paused, wickedly, in the dark for my mother to ask what it meant. All she did was breathe more sternly as if she knew my mind and what I was up to.

Earlier in the day I had stuck up my hand for the very first time. I didn't wave it around like Mabel did. I waited patiently until Mr. Watts nodded. I started in the usual way.

"My name is Matilda."

"Yes, Matilda," said Mr. Watts.

"What is a rimy morning?"

"A rimy morning is a frosty morning. It is a word you don't hear much anymore." He smiled. "Matilda is a nice name, too. Where did you get such a pretty one?" he asked.

"My father."

"And he...?"

I anticipated his question. My dad had worked with

Australians up at the mine. They had given him the name Matilda. He had given it to my mum. And she had given it to me. I explained all this.

"A sort of hand-me-down." Mr. Watts glanced away with the thought. Suddenly he looked gloomy. I don't know why. He turned back to the pages and noticed I had my hand up again.

"Yes, Matilda."

"What is a frosty morning?"

Whenever he considered a question, Mr. Watts' gaze explored the back wall or journeyed to the open window, as if the answer could be found there. This time he put the question to the class. "Can anyone tell me what a frosty morning is?"

Nobody could. We were amazed when he told us the truth of a rimy morning. We could not imagine air so cold that it made smoke come out of your mouth or caused grass to snap in your hands. We could not imagine such a world. None of us kids had tasted anything cold for months, since the last generator had stopped working. For us something cold was something left in the shade or buffed by the night air.

A rimy morning. I waited for my mum to bite. But that bait didn't interest her. She didn't care what a rimy morning was. Or else she didn't want to appear dumb or backwards. So when her question didn't come I brought her up to date with events more pleasing to her. The sight of the old convict chomping into the food like a dog. And the possibility of the police in the kitchen when Pip arrives home. She was especially pleased about that. In the dark I heard her smack her lips.

But that was the last time she asked to hear an installment from *Great Expectations*. And I blame "a rimy morning." Although she didn't say so, I knew she thought I was showing off and that I was biting off a bigger piece of the world than she could handle with language like "a rimy morning." She didn't want to encourage me by asking questions. She didn't want me to go deeper into that other world. She worried she would lose her Matilda to Victorian England.

AROUND DAWN WE HEARD THE REDSKINS' helicopters pass over the village and then return. They hovered in the air like giant dragonflies, peering down at the clearing. They saw a line of abandoned houses and an empty beach because we had cleared off. Everyone. The old people. Mums and dads. The kids. And those dogs and chickens that had names. We hid in the jungle and waited. We waited until we heard the helicopters beat over the treetops. We could feel the breeze their blades sent down. I remember looking around our huddled group and wondering where Mr. Watts and Grace were.

We kept under the trees and followed a bush track back to the village. The dogs that had been too old and skinny to move from their favorite places lifted their snouts. The roosters strutted around. Seeing them made you feel human, because they didn't know anything. They didn't know about guns and the redskins from Moresby. They didn't know about the mine or about the politics or of our fears. The roosters only knew how to be roosters.

The helicopters had gone but we were left with our fear. We didn't know what to do with it. We walked around. We stood in doorways. We stared off into space. Then, one by one, we realized there was nothing else to do but return to our normal routine. That meant school.

Mr. Watts stood at the front of the class as we filed in. I waited until the last of the kids had slid into their desks before I stuck up my hand. I asked him if he had heard the helicopters, and if so, where had he and Mrs. Watts hidden themselves. It was the question we had all brought to school.

Our faces seemed to amuse Mr. Watts. He jiggled a pencil in his palm. "We didn't hide, Matilda," he said. "Mrs. Watts wasn't up to an early morning excursion. As for myself, I like to use that hour for reading." And that was that.

"Will we have the pleasure of your mother in class today, Matilda?" he asked.

"Yes," I said, and tried hard not to sound so unhappy about it.

As it turned out, another mum got the times confused and turned up. She was married to Wilson Masoi, a fisherman, and their son Gilbert came to class only if his father decided he wouldn't go fishing. She was a large woman. She came through the doorway side-on. The boy with the big woolly head who sat in front of me was Gilbert. Today I could see right over the top of him because he was slumped over his desk, ashamed to see his mother in class.

It didn't escape Mr. Watts' attention. He looked toward the back of the class as if he had forgotten something. "Gilbert. Would you like to introduce your mother to the class?"

Gilbert winced. He bit the insides of his cheeks. Slowly he gathered himself up. He managed to stand, but with his chin attached to his chest, his eyes trying to poke through the top of his eyelids. We heard him mutter, "This is Mum."

"Oh, come now, Gilbert," said Mr. Watts. "Does Mum have a name?"

"Mrs. Masoi."

"Mrs. Masoi. Thank you, Gilbert. You may sit down."

Mr. Watts conferred with Gilbert's mum. As he did so, he took a light hold of Mrs. Masoi's elbow. She had a big head of black cotton hair. She was barefoot and her shapeless white dress was filthy. As they ended their private conversation I heard Mr. Watts say, "Jolly good." And to the rest of us he announced, "Mrs. Masoi has some cooking tips to share."

Gilbert's mum turned to face us. She closed her eyes and recited: "To kill an octopus, bite it above the eyes. When cooking a turtle, place it shell down first." She looked across to Mr. Watts, who nodded for her to continue. She closed her eyes a second time. "To kill a pig, get two fat uncles to place a board across its throat."

After the pig recipe she opened her eyes and looked to Mr. Watts. He tried to make a joke and asked how big those uncles should be. Mrs. Masoi answered, "Fat ones. Fat is good. Skinny no bloody good." Poor Gilbert. He was wincing, and shuffling his big behind in the desk in front of me.

*

THE NEXT MORNING we woke to the helicopters again. My mum was bent over me, her face pinched with panic. She was yelling at me to hurry. I could hear people shouting outside, and the beating of the blades. Dust and bits of leaves flew in the open window. My mum threw my clothes at me. Outside, people were running in all directions.

I reached the edge of the bush with my mum pulling me deeper and deeper into the trees. We knew the helicopters had landed because the sound of their blades was even. Everywhere in the shadows I saw sweating faces. We tried to blend in with the stillness of the trees. Some stood. Others crouched; those mums with little ones crouched. They stuck their teats into the mouths of their babies to shut them up. No one spoke. We waited and waited. We sat still. Our faces dripped sweat. We waited until we heard the helicopters beat overhead into the distance. Even then we waited until Gilbert's father came back to give the all clear. Slowly we picked our way out of the jungle and walked back to our houses.

In the clearing the sun beat down on our dead animals. Chooks and roosters sprawled on their swollen sides. Their heads lay elsewhere in the dust, and it was hard to know which head went where. The same machete blows that took their heads cut down washing and garden stakes.

An old dog had its belly ripped open. We stared at that dog, and thought about a story Gilbert's father had brought from further up the coast where most of the fighting was going on. Now we knew what a human being split open would look like. There was no need to wonder anymore. To stare at that black dog was to see your sister or brother or mum or dad in that same state. You saw how disrespectful the sun could be, and how dumb the palms were to flutter back at the sea and up at the sky. The great shame of trees is that they have no conscience. They just go on staring.

Mabel's dad picked up the dog, and while he held it dripping in his arms he yelled at a boy to come and help stuff the insides back where they belonged. The two of them walked to the edge of the jungle and turfed it into the shadows. The dog's name was Black.

Our prized possession—a goat—had disappeared. If she'd been chopped up we'd have found her entrails. We looked in the jungle. One or two promising paths ended in waterfalls or screens of jungle. The redskins must have taken her with them. In our heads we worked out how this would have been done.

We saw a rope, no, two ropes—hindquarter and forequarter—slung around the beast. We saw it airlifted. We saw its big eyes fill with wonder for the treetops it had never seen suddenly appear below. We tried to imagine what it would feel like to be a goat and have the feeling of lightness tickling its hooves.

⁂

THE BLOCKADE WAS IMPOSED in the first half of 1990. We thought it would be just a matter of time before the outside world came to help us. *Patience* was the word we heard whispered. But now look at what had happened. The wrong people had found us.

We didn't care about the chooks and roosters so much. We could eat fish, and the trees dripped with fruit. It was Black and his insides exposed to the harsh sun that we thought about.

My mum came and spoke to the class later that same day. She didn't warn me. I had no idea what she would talk about. She didn't know anything outside of what she knew from the Bible.

Just as he had with Gilbert, Mr. Watts hunted me out with his large eager eyes. "Matilda, would you like to do the honors?"

I stood up and announced what everyone already knew. "This is my mum."

"And does Mum have a name?"

"Dolores," I said, and slid lower into my desk. "Dolores Laimo."

My mum smiled back at me. She was wearing the green scarf my dad had sent in the very last package we received. She wore it tied tight at the back of her head, which was the same way the rebels wore their bandannas. Her hair was pulled back in a tight bun. It gave her an air of defiance. Her mouth clamped down, her nostrils flared. My father used to say she had the blood of righteousness running in her veins. She should have been a churchwoman, he'd say, because persuasiveness for my mum was not an intellectual exercise. Quality of argument was neither here nor there. It was all about the intensity of belief. And every part of her—from the whites of her eyes to her muscular calves—rallied on her behalf.

My mum didn't smile enough. When she did it was nearly always in victory. Or else it was at nighttime when she thought she was all alone. When she was thinking she tended to look angry, as if the act of thinking was potentially ruinous, even ending in her humiliation. Even when she concentrated she looked angry. In fact, she appeared to be angry much of the time. I used to think it was because she was thinking about my dad. But she couldn't have been thinking about him all the time.

She knew the contents of what she called the Good Book. She thought about those contents a lot. And I wouldn't have thought there was anything in that book to make her angry, but that's how she appeared, and why a lot of the kids found her scary.

She must have anticipated this because she used her softer voice, the one I used to hear in the night before *Great Expectations* came between us.

"Children, I have come to talk to you about faith," she said. "You must believe in something. Yes, you must. Even the palm trees believe in the air. And the fish believe in the sea."

As she cast her eye around the room she began to empty her mind of the only subject she trusted, and knew, and cared anything about.

"When the missionaries came, we were taught to have faith in God. But when we asked to see God the missionaries refused to introduce us. Many of the old people preferred to stay with the wisdom of crabs, and the filefish that is shaped like the Southern Star, because if you were to swim with your head down you could swim from one island to another just by taking your bearings from the filefish. What do you kids think of that, eh?"

She leaned forward. Mr. Watts might as well not have been present.

"It's better to have the company of filefish, don't you think? If you did, then you could say your survival was simply a matter of faith, which is what one old fisherman, rescued from his sunken canoe, told my father when I was a girl. At night he knew where he was by the stars. During the day he kept his face in the water and followed the filefish. This is true."

None of us was about to dispute it. The others sat rigid in their desks. The fear I felt from them made me a little embarrassed.

My mum gave a satisfied grunt. She had us where she wanted us. We were that shoal of petrified fish that a shark circles. She slowly straightened up out of her lean, as if taking care not to disturb her effect on us all.

"Now listen. Faith is like oxygen. It keeps you afloat at all times. Sometimes you need it. Sometimes you don't. But when you do need it you better be practiced at having faith, otherwise it won't work. That's why the missionaries built all the churches. Before we got those churches we weren't practicing enough. That's what prayers are for—practice, children. Practice.

"Now, here are some words to learn off by heart. 'In the beginning God created the heaven and the earth... And the earth was without form, and void: and darkness *was* upon the face of the deep. And the spirit of God moved upon the face of the waters.'" My mum's face opened to a rare smile. She found me in the desk up the back and held my eye. "'And God said, Let there be light: and there was light.'"

"There is no sentence in the world more beautiful than that one."

I was aware of several heads turning my way, as if I might beg to differ. Fortunately I was saved by Violet, who had her hand up. She wanted my mum to talk about the wisdom of crabs. At last my mum turned to Mr. Watts.

"Please," he said.

"Crabs," she said, and raised her gaze to the geckos on the ceiling. But she did not see them. Her mind was fastened to crabs, and in particular, to the sort of weather we can expect by looking at the behavior of crabs.

"Wind and rain are on the way if a crab digs straight down and blocks the hole with sand, leaving marks like sunrays. We can expect strong winds but no rain if a crab leaves behind a pile of sand but does not cover the hole.

"If the crab blocks the hole but does not scrape the mound flat there will be rain but no wind. When the crab leaves the sand piled up and the hole unblocked the weather will be fine. Never trust a white who says, 'According to the radio rain is on the way.' Trust crabs first and above all others."

My mum glanced over at Mr. Watts, who laughed to show what a good sport he was.

I wished she could have found it in herself to laugh with him. Instead, she gave him an unfriendly nod to show she was finished with us, and swept out of the class into the afternoon furnace where birds squawked without a memory for the dead dog and the chopped roosters they had seen earlier in the day.

When school finished some of us went down to the beach to look for crabs, to see if what my mum had said was true. We found some unblocked holes, which was proof enough for the boys, but all you had to do was look up at the clear blue skies to find the weather. I wasn't really interested in crabs.

I picked up a stick and in big letters scratched PIP into the sand. I did it above the high-tide line and stuck white heart seeds into the groove of the letters of his name.

The trouble with *Great Expectations* is that it's a one-way conversation. There's no talking back. Otherwise I would have told Pip about my mum coming to speak to the class, and how, seeing her at a distance—even though only two desks back from the end of the room—she had appeared different to me. More hostile.

When she dug in her heels all her heft raced to the surface of her skin. It was almost as if there were friction between her skin and the trailing air. She walked slowly, like a great sail sheet of resistance. She'd put her smile away, and that was a shame because I knew it to be a beautiful smile. There were nights when I saw the moonlight catch the tips of her teeth and I'd know then that she was lying in the dark with a smile. And by that smile I knew she had entered another world, one which I couldn't reach—an adult world and, beyond that, a private world where she knew herself how only *she* and no one else could, let alone follow her there in back of those beautiful moonlit teeth.

Whatever I might say about my mum to Pip I knew he wouldn't hear me. I could only follow him through some strange country that contained marshes and pork pies and people who spoke in long and confusing sentences. Sometimes, by the time Mr. Watts reached the end, you were no better off, you had no sense of what those sentences were trying to say, and maybe by then you were also paying too much attention to the geckos on the ceiling. But then the story would switch to Pip, to his voice, and suddenly you felt yourself reconnect.

As we progressed through the book something happened to me. At some point I felt myself enter the story. I hadn't been assigned a part—nothing like that; I wasn't identifiable on the page, but I was there, I was definitely there. I knew that orphaned white kid and that small, fragile place he squeezed into between his awful sister and lovable Joe Gargery, because the same space came to exist between Mr. Watts and my mum. And I knew I would have to choose between the two.

THE REDSKINS' VISIT AFFECTED US IN DIFferent ways. Some of us were seen hiding food in the jungle. Others made escape plans. They thought about where to escape, and considered what they would do there. My mum's response was to reach for our family history and pass on to me all that she knew.

Sea gods and turtles passed in and out of a long list of people I had never heard of. The names went in one ear and out the other. There were so many. At last she reached the end, or I thought she had. There was a pause. I looked across in the dark and saw the whites of her teeth.

"Pop Eye," she said, "is the offspring of a shining cuckoo."

I knew about the shining cuckoo. At a certain time of the year we saw them leave our skies. They were headed for the nests of strangers to the south. There they find a nest and boot out the eggs of the host bird and lay their own eggs before flying off. The chick of the shining cuckoo never meets its mother.

In the dark I heard my mum click her teeth. She thought she had Mr. Watts summed up. She could not see what us kids had come to see: a kind man. She only saw a white man. And white men had stolen her husband and my father. White men were to blame for the mine, and the blockade. A white man had given us the name of our island. White men had given me my name. By now it was also clear that the white world had forgotten us.

JUST BEFORE CHRISTMAS, TWO MORE BABIES died of malaria. We buried them and marked their graves with white shells and stones carried up from the beach. All night we listened to the mothers wailing.

Their grief turned our thoughts back to a conflict few of us kids properly understood. We knew about the river pollution, and the terrible effect of the copper tailings after heavy rain. Fishermen spoke of a reddish stain that pushed out far beyond the reef into open sea. You only had to hate that to hate the mine. And there were other issues that took me years to grasp: the pitiful amount paid to the lessees by the mining company; and the *wontok* system of the redskins, who had arrived on our island in large numbers to work for the company, and who used their position to advance their own kind, elbowing the locals out of jobs.

In our village there were those who supported the rebels—my mum included. Though I suspect her support was nourished by the thought of my father in Townsville living what she called a "fat life." Everyone else just wished the fighting would go away, and for the white man to come back and reopen the mine. These people missed buying things. They missed having money to buy those things. Biscuits, rice, tinned fish, tinned beef, sugar. We were back to eating what our grandparents had—sweet potatoes, fish, chicken, mango, guava, cassava, nuts, and mud crab.

The men wanted beer. Some men brewed jungle juice and got drunk. We'd hear their drunken carry-on through the night. Their wild behavior was so loud, we were afraid they would be heard by the redskins. In the dark I heard my mum condemn them to hell for their foul language. Jungle juice turned them crazy. They sounded like men who wouldn't care if the world ended tomorrow, and they shocked the night with their ranting.

But this night we heard a different voice, a voice of reason. The wild drunken cries fell away to a single calm voice. I recognized it. It belonged to Mabel's dad; this quiet man with a flat nose and calm, listening eyes. Whenever he saw Mabel he tugged on one of her pigtails and laughed. A happy man. He must also have had some power because in the dead of night we heard him talk to the drunks. He did not raise his voice, so we did not hear what was said, but we heard its calm flow and soon, to our amazement, we heard one of the drunks begin to sob. Just like that. Mabel's dad had talked a raving drunk man down into a sobbing child.

⁂

WHAT DID I HOPE FOR? Just hope itself, really, but in a particular way. I knew things could change because they had for Pip.

First, he is invited by the wealthy Miss Havisham up to her house to play cards with her adopted girl, Estella. I never took to Estella. I can say now that I was jealous of her. I didn't like that other teasing girl, Sarah Pocket, either. I was always glad when it came time to leave Miss Havisham's.

In *Great Expectations* we learned how a life could change without any warning. Pip is into the fourth year of his apprenticeship with Joe Gargery. So he has leaped ahead of me in age. But this didn't matter. In other respects he stayed a true friend, a companion I worried about and thought of lots.

He will become a blacksmith, it seems. A *blacksmith*. There was another word to ask about. Mr. Watts said it was more than a job. By *blacksmith* Mr. Dickens meant more than a man hammering horseshoes into shape. Pip has settled into the routines that go with the blacksmith's life, including nights huddled around the fire with Joe Gargery and others at a pub with the funny name of Three Jolly Bargemen, drinking ale and listening to one another's nonsense.

One night a stranger enters the pub and asks to have Pip pointed out to him. This is Mr. Jaggers, a lawyer from London. He seemed a brave man to us kids. A man unafraid to walk into a group of strangers and start waving his finger about. He asks Pip for a private conference. So Joe and Pip bring him back to the house, and there Mr. Jaggers declares his interest. He has some news for Pip. His life is about to change.

The reading stumbled around these new words as Mr. Watts had to explain what a lawyer was, as well as the word *benefactor*—which led to the word *beneficiary*. That was the lawyer's news. Pip was the beneficiary of a lot of money set aside by someone who wished to keep their identity a secret. The money would be used to turn Pip into a gentleman. So he was about to change *into* something.

When I first heard that I fretted to the end of the chapter. I needed to see what he would change into before I could be sure we would remain friends. I didn't want him to change.

Mr. Watts then talked about what it was to be a gentleman. Though it meant many things, he thought the word *gentleman* best described how a man should be in the world. "A gentleman is a man who never forgets his manners, no matter the situation. No matter how awful, or how difficult the situation."

Christopher Nutua had his hand up.

"Can a poor person be a gentleman?" he asked.

"A poor person most certainly can," said Mr. Watts. He was usually tolerant of our questions, even of our dumbest questions, but this one made him testy. "Money and social standing don't come into it. We are talking about qualities. And those qualities are easily identified. A gentleman will always do the right thing."

We understood what had been revealed, and that it was Mr. Watts' personal conviction. He glanced around the class. As there were no more questions he resumed reading, and I listened carefully.

The money meant Pip would get to leave behind everything he'd known—the marshes, his rotten sister, dear old rambling Joe, the blacksmith's forge—for the big, unknown city of London.

By now I understood the importance of the forge in the book. The forge was home: it embraced all those things that give a life its shape. For me, it meant the bush tracks, the mountains that stood over us, the sea that sometimes ran away from us; it was the ripe smell of blood I could not get out of my nostrils since I saw Black with its belly ripped open. It was the hot sun. It was the fruits we ate, the fish, the nuts. The noises we heard at night. It was the earthy smell of the makeshift latrines. And the tall trees, which like the sea sometimes looked eager to get away from us. It was the jungle and its constant reminder of how small you were, and how unimportant, compared to the giant trees and their canopy's greed for sunlight. It was the laughter of the women in the streams with their washing. It was their joking, teasing delight in discovering a girl secretly washing her rags. It was fear, and it was loss.

Away from class I found myself wondering about the life my dad was leading, and what he had become. I wondered if he was a gentleman, and whether he had forgotten all that had gone into making him. I wondered if he remembered me, and if he ever thought about my mum. I wondered if the thought of us kept him awake at night like the thought of him did her.

⁂

I SAT WATCHING my mum wash our clothes in a hill stream. She beat the dirt out against a smooth rock, then soaked the bruised cloth in the water, shook it out, and let it float.

I had been keeping my distance. It was my way of punishing her for having been rude to Mr. Watts. Now I thought of another way of getting at her. I took aim at the back of her head and asked her if she missed my dad. No angry look flashed over her shoulder, which is what I had expected. No. What happened was her hands became busier. So did her shoulders.

"Why do you ask, girl?"

I shrugged, but of course she didn't see that. A new silence was about to open up between us.

"Sometimes," she added. "Sometimes I will look up and see the jungle part, and there is your father, Matilda. And he is walking towards me."

"And me?"

She dropped the washing and turned to me.

"And you. Yes. Your father is walking towards us both. And then I have memories."

"Which are?"

"No blimmin' use," she said. "That's what they are. But since you ask, I do remember back when the mine was open and your father was in court on a disorderly charge."

I didn't know any of this, and yet her tone of voice suggested my father's misdemeanor was no worse, say, than his forgetting to bring her something home from Arawa. His court appearance was no more calamitous than an instant of forgetfulness. This is what she wished me to believe. But I didn't. I wished she hadn't told me. There was more.

"I remember how soft and red his face looked," she said. "How very sorry in a pray-to-God-I-am-sorry sort of way. Well, I remember looking out the window of the courthouse. I saw an airplane draw a white line in the sky, and at the same time a coconut fell past the window. For a moment, I did not know which one to look at, eh—at that thing that was rising or the thing that was falling."

She pushed off her knees and stood up so she could look at me.

"If you really must know, Matilda, I didn't know if I was looking at a bad man or a man who loved me."

I was hearing more than I wanted. This was adult talk. And because she was watching me carefully I knew she had caught up with that thought.

"I miss sea horses too," she said more brightly. "You will never find a more wise eye anywhere than in a sea horse. This is true. I made that discovery when I was younger than you. And I discovered something about parrot fish. They stare at you in their hundreds and actually remember you from the day before and the day before that one."

"That's a lie." I laughed.

"No," she said. "It's true." She held her breath, and so did I, and she was the first to burst out laughing.

Now that I had met Miss Havisham, and knew more about her unhappy past, I had changed my mind about my mum being like Pip's sister. She had more in common with

Miss Havisham—Miss Havisham who cannot move on from the day of her greatest disappointment. On the clock, the exact hour and minute that the bridegroom failed to show. The wedding feast untouched, left for the cobwebs to mark time.

Miss Havisham remains in her wedding gown for an event that has been and gone. I had an idea my mum was stuck in a similar moment. Only it had to do with an argument with my dad. Her frown gave her away. A frown that could be traced back to the original moment. I had an idea that whatever my dad had said still rang in her ears.

YOU CANNOT BE ANY MORE STUCK THAN the only white person living among black people. Mr. Watts was another I regarded as stuck. He had given us Pip, and I had come to know this Pip as if he were real and I could feel his breath on my cheek. I had learned to enter the soul of another. Now I tried to do the same with Mr. Watts.

I watched his face and I listened to his voice and I tried to hear how his mind ticked, and what he thought. What was Mr. Watts thinking as our mums and dads, our uncles and aunts, and sometimes an older brother or sister came to share with the class what they knew of the world? He liked to position himself to one side as our visitor delivered their story or anecdote or theory.

We always watched Mr. Watts' face for a sign that what we were hearing was nonsense. His face never gave such a sign. It displayed a respectful interest, even when Daniel's grandmother, stooped and old on her canes, peered back at our class with her weak eyes.

"There is a place called Egypt," she said. "I know nothing of that place. I wish I could tell you kids about Egypt. Forgive me for not knowing more. But if you care to listen, I will tell you everything I know about the color blue."

And so we heard about the color blue.

"Blue is the color of the Pacific. It is the air we breathe. Blue is the gap in the air of all things, such as the palms and iron roofs. But for blue we would not see the fruit bats. Thank you, God, for giving us the color blue.

"It is surprising where the color blue pops up," continued Daniel's grandmother. "Look and ye shall find. You can find blue squinting up in the cracks of the wharf at Kieta. And you know what it is trying to do? It is trying to get at the stinking fish guts, to take them back home. If blue was an animal or plant or bird, it would be a seagull. It gets its sticky beak into everything.

"Blue also has magical powers," she said. "You watch a reef and tell me if I am lying. Blue crashes onto a reef and what color does it release? It releases white! Now, how does it do that?"

Our eyes sought out Mr. Watts for an explanation, but he pretended not to notice our questioning faces. He sat on the edge of the desk, his arms folded. Every part of him looked to be focused on what Daniel's grandmother had to say. One by one our attention shifted back to the little old woman with the betel-stained mouth.

"A final thing, children, and then I will let you go. Blue belongs to the sky and cannot be nicked, which is why the missionaries stuck blue in the windows of the first churches they built here on the island."

Mr. Watts did that now-familiar thing of opening his eyes wide as if waking from a sleep. He walked over to Daniel's grandmother with an outstretched hand. The old woman gave hers for him to hold, then he turned to the class.

"Today, we have been very lucky. Very lucky. We have received a handy reminder that while we may not know the whole world, we can, if we are clever enough, make it new. We can make it up with the things we find and see around us. We just have to look and try to be as imaginative as Daniel's grandmother." He put a hand on the shoulder of the old woman. "Thank you," he said. "Thank you so much."

Daniel's grandmother grinned back at the class and we saw how few teeth she had left, and the few she did have explained why she whistled when she spoke.

Others who came to speak to the class had to be persuaded by Mr. Watts to give up what they knew, and in some cases it was very little.

The woman who had owned Black dropped her shy eyes to the ground. And when Giselle spoke, Mr. Watts had to lean towards her to catch what she said about wind. "Some islands have beautiful names for different winds. My favorite is the wind that is known as 'gentle as a woman.'"

Gilbert's uncle, a big man, round as an oil drum, black as tar from toiling out at sea, came to speak to us about "broken dreams." He said the best place to find a broken dream is on the wharf. "Look at all those dead fish with their eyes and mouths open. They can't believe they are not in the sea and never will be again."

He stopped to look at Mr. Watts, as if to ask, Is this the sort of thing you're after? Mr. Watts gave a nod, and Gilbert's uncle continued.

"At night the blimmin' dogs and roosters chase after dreams and break them in two. The one good thing about a broken dream is that you can pick up the threads of it again. By the way, fish go to heaven. Don't believe any other shit you hear."

He shifted from one bare foot to the other, tilting his nervous eyes to Mr. Watts, then back at us. "That's all I've got for now," he said.

We heard about an island where the kids sit in a stone canoe and learn sacred sea chants by heart. We heard you can sing a song to make an orange tree grow. We heard about songs that worked like medicine. For example, you can sing a certain one to get rid of hiccups. There are even songs to get rid of sores and boils.

We learned about remedies, such as placing the leaves of white lilies on sores. There was another scrubby plant whose long green leaves were good for earache. Leaves of another plant could be squeezed and drunk to cure diarrhea. Kina shells should be boiled for soup and fed to first-time mothers to stop the bleeding.

Some stories will help you find happiness and truth. Some stories teach you not to make the same mistake twice. These ones offer instruction. Look here to the Good Book.

A woman called May told a story about a frigate bird

that had brought her a birthday card from a neighboring island. The card was folded inside an old toothpaste box that was taped under the bird's wing. It was for her eighth birthday and the large bird seemed to know this because, she said, it stood with her mum and dad watching her as she read the note, and when she came to the words "Happy birthday, May," she said everyone cheered and that's when she saw the bird smile.

"The next day we ate it for my birthday lunch."

When Mr. Watts heard that, his head reared back and his arms dropped to his sides. He looked appalled. I wonder if May noticed, because she then said, "Of course, the bird didn't know about that part."

Still, we all felt uncomfortable because Mr. Watts had been made to feel uncomfortable.

One old woman stood before us and shouted, "Ged up, you lazybones! Get off your arses and follow the seabirds out to the fishing grounds." It was a traditional story.

Another woman from my mum's prayer group came to talk to us about good manners. "Silence is an indicator of good manners," she said. "When I was growing up, silence was the bits left over after the blimmin' dogs and the blimmin' roosters and the generators had had a go at the world. Most of us kids didn't know what to do with it. Sometimes we mistook silence for being bored. But silence is good for a lot of things—sleeping, being at one with God, thinking about the Good Book.

"Also," she added, waving a finger at us girls in the class, "stay away from boys who abuse silence. Boys who shout have mud in their souls. A man who knows about the wind and sailing a boat also knows about silence and is likely to be more sensitive to the presence of God. Other than that, I don't want to tell you girls where to shop."

Agnes Haripa began her talk on sex with a smile. She didn't speak until she had every one of us smiling back at her. Gilbert was slow to respond and she stood patiently smiling at him for some time before Mr. Watts intervened and asked Gilbert if he was going to oblige. To help Gilbert, Mr. Watts produced a smile of his own. "Oh yeah," said Gilbert, and Mrs. Haripa was able to get on with her lesson.

"Today I wish to speak on what the lychee can teach us," she said. "Sweet things are never worn on the outside." She held up a spiky lychee for all of us to see, as if none of us had ever set eyes on this fruit. We knew about its thin hard shell. You peeled it off and sank your teeth into its creamy-textured, almond-tasting flesh. "But like a lychee," continued Agnes, "a person's sweet smile says nothing about a person's heart. A smile can be a trick. To stay sweet you have to protect yourself. Girls, protect your sweets from the boys. Look at the lychee. Would it taste so sweet if its fruits were exposed to the sun and the rains and the longing of dogs?"

We caught on. We knew what she wanted and chanted back, "No, Mrs. Haripa."

"No," she said. "Them fruits would dry up and shrivel. They'd lose their sweetness, which is why the lychee's sweet part sits behind a hard shell. Everyone knows this to be true, but hardly anyone ever asks why. Now you kids know."

She made another sweeping inspection of our faces. She was looking for a troublemaker, someone who might have a question. Questions were all right so long as you knew what seeded a question. Was the question a genuine attempt to find something out or was it to trip you up? Mrs. Haripa was a friend of my mum's. They belonged to the same prayer group.

"I don't think there are any questions, Mrs. Haripa," said Mr. Watts, to our great relief. "However, if I may say so, I found your talk on the preservation of innocence very affecting."

Mrs. Haripa's eyes blazed at Mr. Watts. She wasn't sure if the white man was making fun of her. What was that smile hiding? Some white cunning? And these kids knew his masks better than she did. Why were those kids all of a sudden smiling that way? Perhaps she should have spoken about the cassava or the many uses of chicken feathers.

I was enjoying her discomfort so much I almost missed Mr. Watts' raised eyebrow, which was a cue for me to stand up and thank Mrs. Haripa for her contribution.

The class broke into polite applause and then Mrs. Haripa nodded happily back at us. And we were happy for her. We wanted our cousins and our mothers and grandmothers to tell us stuff. We didn't want them scared to come to class. But we also saw how shame and a fear of looking stupid was never far from the surface, and this is what kept some at a distance; these ones made it as far as the clearing before doubt made a skittery run across their hearts. Marooned by doubt and unable to come closer for wondering if their story of the gecko was important enough to share. Then we might look up in time to catch the back view of someone fleeing across the open ground for the trees.

An aunt of Mabel's turned up with a woven mat. She had come to talk about "directions and luck." "Weavings can tell you a thing or two," she said. "My grandmother wove me a sleeping mat in case I got lost in my dreams. All I had to do was roll over until I felt a raised seam. That seam was the current that would deliver me home.

"She also told me a story about a young woman who carried the knowledge of the tides and sea currents inside of her body. Then she made up a song about the various directions a person can take. My niece was given such a mat as this one I hold in my hands. She was to sing her way from the airport to her other aunt's house in Brisbane. I heard later she forgot the song and left the mat in the toilet. In any case, her aunt and cousins turned up at the airport."

My mum even returned to speak of things I had never heard her say before. Mr. Watts stationed himself behind her. I thought he looked nervous. He fidgeted, and his gaze couldn't settle in one place.

"Women were never allowed to go to sea—ever!" she barked. "Why not? I will tell you why, even though it is obvious to the thickest tree trunk. Women are too valuable. That is why. So the fellas went. If a woman was to go, look at what might be lost—there would be no babies, no food on the table, and the noise of the sweeping broom would be lost forever. Plus, the island would starve to death.

"But, sometimes, and this is according to my aunt Josephine, if you saw a young woman standing on a reef following the flight of a seabird, it was a sure thing she had lost her virginity and she had it in her head to strike out to the nearest white man's city. So if you girls look at the seabirds you had better do it from the beach or bloody watch out!"

IT WAS ALWAYS A RELIEF TO RETURN TO *Great Expectations*. It contained a world that was whole and made sense, unlike ours. If it was a relief for us, then what must it have been for Mr. Watts? I feel equally sure he was more comfortable in the world of Mr. Dickens than he was in our black-faced world of superstition and mythic flying fish. In *Great Expectations* he was back among white people.

Sometimes as he read we saw him smile privately, leaving us to wonder why, at that particular moment—only to realize yet again that there were parts of Mr. Watts we could not possibly know because of our ignorance of where he'd come from, and to reflect on what he'd given up in order to join Grace on our island.

Whenever I walked near Mr. Watts' desk I tried not to look too obviously at the book sitting there. I was dying to pick it up and gaze at the words and locate Pip's name on the page. But I didn't want to reveal my desire. I didn't want to reveal a part of myself that I thought of as private, and possibly even shameful. I was still mindful of Mrs. Haripa's lesson on the lychee.

Outside the class we were seeing more of Mr. Watts. We saw him wander among the trees with a basket to pick fruits. Some of the parents gave him and Mrs. Watts food as a thank-you for his stocking our empty heads every day. Gilbert's father always had a fish left over for Mr. Watts.

He saved his white linen suit for school, and that's how we saw him most of the time, as a "gentleman." To see him on the beach in his baggy old shorts with a plastic bucket was to wonder what had happened to Mr. Watts of the classroom. You saw how terribly thin he had become or really was, which was akin to making a discovery—I couldn't be sure of which. He looked like a skinny white vine. To see him so stooped was to realize the special effort he made to dress and stand tall in class. On the beach, though, he was like the rest of us. Head down, alert to whatever had washed up. He wore an old white shirt, which, unusually, he had left unbuttoned, but as he drew nearer I saw it had lost all its buttons.

I had collected a basket of cowrie shells and was adding these to the heart seeds to make PIP even more visible, when Mr. Watts looked up from his beachcombing. He saw me and left the water's edge to walk up the sand.

"A shrine," he said approvingly. "Pip in the Pacific." He thought about that. "Well, who knows? He might well have made it here. *Great Expectations* doesn't tell the whole of Pip's life. The book ends..." He stopped when he saw me place my hands against my ears.

I didn't want to be told. I wanted to hear from the book. I wanted to move at the book's pace. I didn't want to jump ahead. "You are quite right, Matilda. All in good time..."

He was about to add something else, when he frowned. I thought I heard him swear. If he did he muffled it. In the end I wasn't sure if I'd heard correctly and the heat in my cheeks was all for nothing. Balancing on one leg he brought his right foot up to his crotch and studied it. The problem was a flapping toenail on his big toe. He pulled it back on its skinny hinges.

"I expect it will work itself free soon enough," he said, as we stared at the pink flesh that lies behind a toenail. "There are some things you never expect to lose, things you think will forever be part of you, even if it is only a toenail."

"A *big* toenail," I said.

"That's right," he said. "Not just any."

"What will happen when it comes off?"

"I expect another one will grow."

"So that's okay," I said. "Nothing's lost."

"Except that particular toenail," he said. "You could say the same about a house or one's country. No two are the same. You gain as you lose, and vice versa." He stared off distantly, as if everything he'd parted with trailed out to sea and over the horizon. Television. Picture theaters. Cars. Friends. Family. Tinned food. Shops.

Here was my opportunity to ask if he missed the white world, and to ask what he felt he had gained by giving up the chance to leave the island when he could. And did he regret it now?

Of course, my courage failed me. This was the first time I had spoken to Mr. Watts alone and I was very aware of his status as a grown-up and as a white. Besides, our favorite topic was Mr. Dickens, rather than ourselves, so I was happier to shift the conversation from his toenail (and its surprising associations) to *Great Expectations*. I had some matters to raise with Mr. Watts.

I was troubled by what I had detected to be a shift in Pip's personality now that he was in London. I didn't like his London friends. I didn't take to his housemate Herbert Pocket, and I couldn't understand why Pip had, and it worried me that he was leaving me behind. Nor could I understand why he had changed his name to Handel.

Mr. Watts plonked himself down on the sand beside me. He leaned back on his hands and squinted at the sparkling sea.

"Let's see if I can explain, Matilda. This is how I see it, which is not to say it's the only way, but it is my answer to it. Pip is an orphan. He is like an emigrant. He is in the process of migrating from one level of society to another. A change of name is as good as a change of clothes. It is to help him on his way."

I was stuck on the word *emigrant*. To ask Mr. Watts its meaning, though, would be a risk. Mr. Watts' approach assumed a shared intelligence. And while that was flattering it was also intimidating. I didn't want to disappoint Mr. Watts. I didn't want to say anything that might rock his faith in me. So I moved on to another thing that troubled me—Pip's treatment of Joe Gargery.

First, his embarrassment when Joe turns up in London unannounced. Pip acts in a superior way to his loyal old blacksmith friend. Then, on his trip home from London, he goes out of his way to avoid Joe. He has only come back to visit Estella. He can't be bothered with Joe anymore.

With Mr. Watts' encouragement I had spoken freely, and was pleased to think I had made an important observation, though it seemed to make him tired.

"It is hard to be a perfect human being, Matilda," he said. "Pip is only human. He has been given the opportunity to turn himself into whomever he chooses. He is free to choose. He is even free to make bad choices."

"Like Estella," I said.

"Oh, you don't like Estella?"

"She's mean."

"That she is," he said. "But we find out why in due course."

Once more I thought he was about to tell me, only to catch himself and glance away with what he knew. There was no hurry for the information. We had all eternity in front of us. If we were in any doubt about that we had only to look out to sea.

Mr. Watts had settled himself in the sand. Now I watched him pick himself up. As he raised himself to his full height he realized, with some annoyance, he had forgotten his bucket. He eyed it for a moment. I could have passed it up to him but I was too engrossed in Mr. Watts' irritation. How hard was it to reach for a plastic bucket?

He placed his free hand on his hip and, as he bent down

for the bucket, his face turned red with the effort. Just for a moment he reverted to Pop Eye. But then as he straightened he filled out to the classroom version I knew. He ironed out an ache in the small of his back and turned to look along the beach.

"Well," he said, "I think I can hear Mrs. Watts calling me."

I watched him walk away with his plastic bucket, a much older man than I'd come to realize. His linen suit and careful classroom manner concealed his frailty. He stopped and looked over his shoulder, as if trying hard to reach a decision about me. He called out, "Matilda, can you keep a secret?"

"Yes," I said quickly.

"You asked about Pip changing his name to Handel."

"Yes," I said.

Mr. Watts returned to where I sat in the sand. He shielded his eyes and gazed up the beach, then in the other direction. He looked at me, and I had the impression he was annoyed for putting himself in the position of telling more. But he had come this far.

"You need to understand. This has to be our secret, Matilda."

"I promise," I said.

"Grace is not my wife's name," he said. "Everyone here knows her as Grace, of course. But she changed it. Her name is Sheba. This happened many years ago, before you were born. Because of certain events, shall we say, and at a time in her life when she needed to make changes, she took the name of Sheba. Because of these difficulties she was having to deal with, I thought—or hoped, really—that she might grow into her name. It happens with other creatures. Once you know the name of that funny little amphibious creature with the helmet, it can't be anything else than a turtle. A cat is a cat. It is impossible to think of a dog as being anything else than a dog. I hoped Sheba might eventually grow into her name."

He looked at me closely. I had an idea he was checking to see how safe this secret would be with me. He needn't have worried. I was thinking about the name Sheba. If *dog* meant dog and could only ever be dog, and *turtle* turtle, what did *Sheba* mean?

"That's it, Matilda. Now you know something no one else on this whole island knows."

He waited, as if expecting something in return. But I didn't have a secret to give him.

"Well, until the next time," he said. He gave me a wink, and wandered off.

THE NEAREST VILLAGE WAS EIGHT KILO-meters up the coast. But we got news from all over the island. It traveled along tracks through the jungle, over mountain passes. And it was never good news. No. We were hearing terrible things. Things we didn't want to believe.

There was talk of redskin reprisals against those villages that cooperated with the rebels. Little kids ran about with stories of people flung out of helicopters onto the treetops. They thought this might be fun, and it might even be something that they would like to try out for themselves. Those little kids were a sign of how loose our parents' talk had become. They still kept back the worst of it. What we didn't hear for ourselves we saw on their worried faces. And just like that, we were taken back to how the dog Black appeared with its sides ripped open.

My mum's prayer meetings were drawing more and more people. God would help us. We just needed to pray more. A prayer was like a tickle. Sooner or later God would have to look down to see what was tickling his bum.

At night my mum maintained a restless silence. She was mentally fending off all that bad news to make space for God. On that subject, she asked if us kids ever heard the word of the Good Lord from Pop Eye.

"Mr. Watts does not use the Bible," I said.

She let that sit in the air, as if it were a betrayal of our very safety. Then she returned to her other preoccupation, testing me with the names of relatives and fish and birds from our family tree.

I failed miserably. I could think of no reason to remember them, whereas I knew the name of every character I had met in *Great Expectations* because I had heard them speak. They had shared their thoughts with me, and sometimes as Mr. Watts read aloud I could even see their faces. Pip, Miss Havisham, and Joe Gargery were more part of my life than my dead relatives, even the people around me.

But Mum was not put off by my repeated failures. She said I should unblock my ears. She said she felt sorry for my heart. My heart, she said, didn't have much of a choice for company. She wouldn't let go of this task she set me. She was insistent. The tests continued, without success. Then she changed strategy. I have an idea she had seen the name PIP on the beach, because one night after I had failed her again she told me to write the names of the family tree in the sand.

The next day I did as she asked—and she came to check on my progress. She became very angry when she saw Pip's name next to the relatives'. She cuffed my hair.

What did I think I was up to? Why did I have to act

dumber than I looked? What was the point of sticking the name of a make-believe person next to her kin?

I knew why. I knew exactly why I had done this. But did I have the courage to stand up for what I believed? I knew from experience you could get four-fifths of your answer right and my mum would pounce on that leftover bit that was wrong. In the end my mouth decided for me. Away it went—leaving me astonished at the way I threw the question back at her.

Now, I asked, where's the value in knowing a few scattered and unreliable facts about dead relatives when you could know all there was to know about a made-up person such as Pip?

She gave me a look of pure hate. She didn't say anything at first. Maybe she was afraid if she opened her mouth too quickly all that would come out would be anger. I waited for the slap. Instead she kicked out at the sand around PIP, then kicked out at the air over his name.

"He isn't a blood relative!" she yelled.

Well, no, Pip wasn't a relative, I explained, but I felt closer to him than the names of those strangers she made me write in the sand. This was not what she wanted to hear. She knew where to place the blame. She looked up the beach in the direction of the old mission house.

The next day Mabel stuck up her hand to ask Mr. Watts if he believed in God.

He looked up at the ceiling; his eyes went searching.

"That is one of those difficult questions I warned the class about," he said. He fiddled with the book in his hands.

He was trying to find our place in *Great Expectations,* but his mind was elsewhere.

Then it was Gilbert's turn to ask. "What about the devil?"

We saw a slow smile creep out onto Mr. Watts' face, and I felt embarrassed for us kids and Mr. Watts because I knew he had just guessed the source of these questions.

"No," he said. "I do not believe in the devil."

This is not something I would have mentioned to my mum. I was not that dumb. One of the other kids must have blabbed, which led to Mr. Watts' heathen beliefs circulating at that evening's prayer meeting.

The following day Mr. Watts was just about to read from *Great Expectations,* when my mum strode into the classroom. She wore the same head wrap she had worn the other time. Now I understood why. It gave her a frightening authority.

Her heavy eyelids drew back and she gave Mr. Watts a hostile look. Then, with a start, she caught sight of the book in his hands. I thought she might try and grab it off him and drive a stake through its covers. Instead she took a deep breath and announced to Mr. Watts she had some informations (she always said "informations") to share with the class.

Mr. Watts politely closed *Great Expectations*. As usual he was guided by his innate sense of courtesy. He gestured for my mum to take the floor and she started in.

"Some white fellas do not believe in the devil or God," she said, "because they think they don't have to. Believe it or not there are some white folk who on the strength of a glance out the window will not pack away a raincoat for their holiday. A white will make sure he has a life jacket in the boat and enough petrol in the tank for a long trip out to sea, but he will not take the same precautions by stocking up on faith for the hurly-burly of daily life."

She bobbed from side to side. She was more cocky than I'd ever seen her.

"Mr. Watts, here, he thinks he is ready for all things. But if this was true, then the man shot by the redskin must be wondering how come he didn't see the helicopter until it was too late. So. But for the rest of us peoples—and that means my beautiful flower, Matilda—pack the teachings of the Good Book into your person. That way you kids can save Mr. Watts because I am not going to be the one."

We looked as one to Mr. Watts to see if he minded. We were glad to find him smiling behind my mum's back. And when she saw us kids smiling too, it made her madder. I was already ashamed by her words, but I also knew her anger didn't really have to do with Mr. Watts' own religious beliefs or lack of. What made her blood run hot was this white boy Pip and his place in my life. For that she held Mr. Watts personally responsible.

If my mum had set out to insult Mr. Watts and show him up, then she failed—if Mr. Watts' smile was anything to go by.

"Once again, Dolores, you have provided us with food for thought," he said.

My mum shot him a look of suspicion. I knew she didn't

know that expression: *food for thought*. She would be wondering if the white man was insulting her without her knowing it. And if that was so, how stupid would she look to us kids?

"I have more," she said.

Mr. Watts kindly gestured for her to carry on, and I sank deeper behind my desk.

"I wish to talk about braids," she announced, and to my horror, she began addressing her remarks to me.

"Matilda, as a young woman your grandmother wore her hair in braids and them braids were thick as rope. Them braids were so strong us kids used to swing on them."

Some of the class laughed, and this encouraged my mum to shift her attention off me.

"This is true. If the tide was up we would hold on to the end of a braid in case we stumbled on coral.

"My mum's braids were so blimmin' long that us kids used to sit in Uncle's wheelchair and hang on to them while her big bum rose above the bike seat. We cheered at that big bum. We hooted like dogs drunk on jungle juice."

This time Mr. Watts laughed along with us kids.

"Now," she said, "the reason for braids is to keep flies off you and to shoo away the boys who want to stick their hands where they shouldn't. A girl who wears braids knows right from wrong—and she's no bloody show-off."

My poor mum. As quickly as she had won us she lost us. And she didn't know why. It was as if she didn't listen to herself.

By the time she arrived at her closing argument we sat

with folded arms and bolted-on expressions of polite interest. "So, when you bring two strands of hair together and tease them into rope you begin to understand the idea of partnership . . . and you understand how God and the devil know each other."

My mum was so eager for us kids to know what she knew, but she didn't know how to plant it in our heads. She thought she could bully us into knowing what she did. Did she notice that whenever she got onto God and the devil, every kid's face dropped? We preferred hearing about dogs drunk on jungle juice.

The moment she left, Mr. Watts knew what to do. He picked up *Great Expectations,* and as he began to read we picked our faces up off our desk lids.

CHRISTMAS DAY. It rained, then the sun burst down on the new puddles. We listened to the croaking of frogs. I saw Celia's little brother Virgil walk by with a frog on the end of a stick. Once I would have asked him to get me a frog. But those things didn't interest me anymore.

There was no school that day, so there was no update on Pip. And there was no feast. That day, of all days, our parents had decided it was too risky to cook. The smoke would give away our position. As if it didn't on any other day. And really, what difference did it make? The redskins knew where we were. So did the rambos, which was the new name for the barefoot rebels who wore bandannas. By now nearly all the young men in the village had joined the rebels, so them we did not fear. But we could tell by the nervous and strained faces of our parents that things were changing, and for us they might change at any moment.

We did not live with quite the same easiness of before. Our heads turned for any unexpected sound. Whenever I heard one of the helicopters I knew what it was to feel your heart stop along with your breath.

There were old people who knew about magic. Some asked for potions to make them invisible for when the redskins came. Others, my mum and most of the mums of the kids in Mr. Watts' class, turned to prayer.

In the tree above the praying women were hundreds of bats hanging upside down. They looked as if they were holding tiny prayerbooks between their wings. It was during one of these prayer meetings, just on dark, that Victoria's older brother Sam staggered out of the jungle. He wore the rebels' bandanna. He carried an old rifle in his hand. He was barefoot and his clothes were ripped. He dragged a wounded leg behind him.

As the prayer group looked up, Sam seemed to realize he was home and allowed himself to fall over. One of us was sent off to fetch Mr. Watts. I wonder if he understood the problem, because he arrived eating a banana.

Once he saw Sam he handed the rest of the banana to me, and he knelt down by him. He gave Sam a drink from a small flask (I heard later it was alcohol), then he rested Sam's head back and fit a piece of wood into his mouth and nodded at Gilbert's father to start hacking. He used a fish knife to dig three redskin bullets out of Sam's leg. He laid the bullets on the grass and we formed a circle around them and stared at them the way we did at a catch of fish laid out on the sand. The bullets were misshapen and a runny color of red.

We didn't like Victoria's brother being here. We were scared the redskins would discover him, which would make us a rebel village. We knew what happened to rebel villages. They were burned down, and had other things done to them that were not spoken aloud around young ears. That was the last time I saw Sam before he was taken into the bush. His mother sat with him day and night, feeding him special roots and water.

Two weeks after Gilbert's father dug the bullets out he took Sam out to sea in his boat. It was nighttime and in the black stillness we could hear the slapping of the oars on the water. Gilbert's father's boat had an outboard, but he didn't want to use the last of his fuel; he was saving that. He was gone for two days. We were asleep when he dragged his boat up on the third night. And when I saw him the next day he did not look the same.

We never saw Sam again.

THE DISTANCE FROM PIP'S HOUSE IN THE marshes to the "metropolis" of London was about five hours. We understood without Mr. Watts saying so that five hours indicated a great distance. In eighteen-hundred-and-fifty-something it might have been. But five hours was nearer than a century and a half and a whole lot closer than half a world away. We heard that Pip was scared of London's "immensity." *Immensity?*

We stared back at Mr. Watts for an explanation. "Sheer numbers, crowds, a sense of bewilderment and of overwhelming scale..." And with the book in hand Mr. Watts' thoughts would drift back to his own experience of London. He spoke about the excitement of his first visit. The smile left his face. I think it was for having the young man he once was in his thoughts. He said everything was vaguely familiar since he had already been led around London by Mr. Dickens.

He spoke of being poor; and of giving an old woman beggar the last of his money and wandering in a park afterwards warmed by the thought of his good deed. Then it had gotten cold. A nasty rain fell and he hurried from the park gates. He waited to cross a busy road. He looked in the lit window of a café and, wishing he had money to buy something, happened to see the old hag buttering a scone, and when she raised her eyes, Mr. Watts said, she looked through him without a flicker of recognition.

We laughed like dogs at our stupid teacher. Mr. Watts nodded. He knew.

He was happy to be the brunt of the joke, but the moment he dropped his eyes to the open pages of *Great Expectations* we shut up. For a moment he didn't read. We had an idea he was back in London with his younger self staring in that lit window—this was one of those moments that reminded us of Mr. Watts' status as the last white man on the island. There he stood before us, one of a kind, with a memory of a place none of us kids had visited or seen or could imagine except in the way supplied by Mr. Dickens.

When we heard the words *metropolis* and *London* our minds drew a blank. Even Mr. Watts' attempts to find a local reference fell flat. He took us down to the beach. There he dug a channel in the sand for the tide to run up. This was the Thames. He found a number of gray rocks and bundled these into one place. These he called buildings. We heard about skylights and coachmen and horsehair, but stopped asking for explanations. We'd learned to recognize the important stuff.

We were meeting Mr. Wemmick, Mr. Jaggers' creepy offsider, for the first time when my mum turned up to class with one of the women from her prayer group. This was

Mrs. Siep. Mrs. Siep's three boys had joined the rebels. Her husband was also thought to have joined them. If he hadn't, then he must be lying dead someplace. Mrs. Siep didn't say.

Mr. Watts vacated his place and my mum gently pushed Mrs. Siep forward and introduced her. Mrs. Siep checked that where she stood was the correct spot. My mum made a small adjustment. We saw Mrs. Siep take a small step back.

"I have two pieces of information to give you kids," announced Mrs. Siep. "The first is about fish bait. You need to catch a remora fish if you wish to catch something bigger. What you do is tie a line around the tail of a remora and it will fish for you—this is the truth, I have seen it with my own eyes. The remora has a sucking disc on top of its head and will use this to attach itself to a shark or turtle or large fish. If you catch a sunfish, cut the line. They are poisonous."

Mrs. Siep inclined her head, and as she took a backwards step we broke into applause. This was new for us, and that we did it without prompting from Mr. Watts says something about the gentlemanly ways we were cultivating under his guidance, as much as Mrs. Siep's dignity. She spoke from some inner calm place that my own mum did not know how to locate.

Mrs. Siep smiled, and as she looked up we ended our applause. She stepped forward once more.

"I will begin with a question. What will you do if you are all alone at sea? This is my second information," she said. "If you are feeling lonely, look out for the triggerfish.

God mixed the souls of dogs and triggerfish together because, like dogs, a triggerfish will roll over on its side and look up at you."

Mrs. Siep inclined her head and for the second time we broke into applause. My mum joined in. I saw her whisper something to Mrs. Siep, who stepped aside for her.

The change in the atmosphere was instant. We braced ourselves.

"I know," she said, "you have been hearing some story from Mr. Watts, and a story in particular, but I want to tell you this. Stories have a job to do. They can't just lie around like lazybone dogs. They have to teach you something. For example, if you know the words you can sing a song to make a fish swim onto your hook. There are even songs to get rid of skin rash and bad dreams. But I want to tell you kids about the devil I met when I was your age. This was back when the church was still here and the mission hadn't moved. We still had the wharf, and the village was much bigger than it is today.

"Well, the first devil I met was back then. I'll tell you kids this just in case I am intersected by a redskin bullet, because you need to know what to look out for, and maybe in this specialist area Mr. Watts is no blimmin' good."

She gave him a quick smile as if to say she was joking. Only I knew she wasn't. She continued.

"This woman, she live by herself, and one day she saw us kids hanging about. She came over and started shouting. *Hey! If you fellas pinched the church money I will pluck your eyelashes out. People will see a plucked chicken and know what you did, that you shitty kids stole the church money.*

"She was scary. We heard she knew magic. She once turned a white man into marmalade and spread him on her toast."

The whole class looked at Mr. Watts. Here was something he might care to challenge. A woman turning a white man into marmalade and spreading him on her toast. Mr. Watts had just heard a ridiculous boast but he gave nothing away. He stood, as he usually did during my mum's performances, with his eyes half-closed and an attentive look on his face.

"So when she asked us kids if we stole the church money we said no, but that was the wrong answer. We could tell that because she looked grumpy. She was thinking what she would say next or maybe she was bored—we couldn't tell, and we thought we could walk away. Then she said, *Well, what if I was to ask you kids to steal the church money?*

"Us boys and girls—we didn't dare look at one another. We would sooner die than steal the church money. If we stole the church money we would die whether we wanted to or not. We weren't going to steal the church money. No way.

"The devil woman read our thoughts because she said, *Listen to me. If I tell you kids to steal the church money you will. And you know why?* Well, none of us did and none of us knew what to say. *No, I thought so, she said, bloody useless kids. Now, watch this.*"

My mum paused, and we all looked at her. She even had Mr. Watts' attention. "I will try to describe what happened next," she said.

"There was a ball of darkness, not quite smoke, that streamed away from where us kids were standing. We covered our eyes and when we dared to look there was a black bird. Though it wasn't a bird any of us had seen before. It had an angry head, the body of a pigeon, and sharp claws, which it used to snatch two small birds, one in each claw. Its beak opened far back and we saw one of its eyes watching us and we knew it was the devil. And while its eye held us kids, it fed one bird into its beak and made a lazy chopping sound, swallowed, and ate the second bird the same way. Then the ugly bird turned into blackness and poured back at our feet. In a blink the ugly woman is back before us with feathers sticking out of her mouth.

"*Now,* she said to us kids, *fetch me the collection from the church next Sunday or else. And don't tell anyone. I will know if you do and I will come for you when you are sleeping on your mats, and I will take your eyeballs and feed them to the fish.*

"We didn't tell our parents because we treasured our eyeballs. And who wants to go blind in the world? But us kids also knew that we stood to commit two crimes. One, we would steal the church money, and two, we'd do something we knew was wrong. So we would be two times wrong. And that darkness would be darker than the dark that comes when you can no longer see. So we did nothing. We let the collection pass under our noses and we did nothing because by Sunday we had decided the lesser darkness would be okay. The devil woman could come and snatch our eyeballs and feed them to the fish.

"We waited all day Sunday for the devil woman to show. And we waited for her to pour through the open window at school the day after. We decided to tell the minister what had happened. He said what we had done was to outwit the devil. He said the devil had been sent to test us kids. That's what the devil is for. To test your convictions. But if we stole the church money, then the woman would have shown up for sure because she'd have had us kids in the palm of the devil's own hand. The minister said, *Well done, you kids,* and gave us each a sweet."

At the end of the story, my mum looked across to Mr. Watts, and the two of them held each other's eye until they remembered us. Had she not done that, us kids would have thought we were hearing a story just about the devil, and we wouldn't have given the redskins a second thought.

*

MY MUM NEVER ASKED me outright how I thought these visits of hers went. She wanted to know: she just came at it from a different angle. That night she asked me if I believed in the devil. Stupidly I answered no. She asked me why—after everything I had been told about the devil—so I recited Mr. Watts' words back to her. I said the devil was a symbol. He isn't living flesh.

"Nor is Pip," she said.

But I had my answer ready. "You cannot hear the devil's voice. You can hear Pip's."

On this point she went quiet. I waited, and I waited, until all I heard back was her gentle snore.

When she showed up in class the next morning it was obvious she hadn't come to speak to us. She had come to pick a fight with Mr. Watts.

"My daughter, my lovely Matilda," she began, "tells me she does not believe in the devil. She believes in Pip."

She stopped to allow Mr. Watts to catch up and say what he wished. As usual he showed no sign of surprise.

"Well, Dolores," he said calmly, "what if we were to say that on the page Pip and the devil have the same status?"

It was Mr. Watts' turn to pause. He waited, but I knew he had lost her.

"Well, let's see," he said. "Pip is an orphan who is given the chance to create his own self and destiny. Pip's experience also reminds us of the emigrant's experience. Each leaves behind the place he grew up in. Each strikes out on his own. Each is free to create himself anew. Each is also free to make mistakes..."

And there my mum saw what she thought was a chink in Mr. Watts' argument.

She held up a hand, and interrupting Mr. Watts she asked him, "But how will he know if he's made a mistake?"

WE FINISHED *GREAT EXPECTATIONS* ON February 10. My calculations were out by four days due to Christmas Day and Mr. Watts taking three days off school to nurse a cold.

I was confused by the book's ending. I didn't understand why Pip would continue to want Estella so much. Especially as I understood her role in the scheme of things. Miss Havisham had put a stone in place of her heart. And that stone was the forge for Estella to break other men's hearts. It was Miss Havisham's payback for what had happened to her on her wedding day. I understood that part—we all knew about payback. And Magwitch, the escaped convict—while I very much liked and admired the idea of his payback to Pip, his getting rich in Australia to pay for the boy to escape the marshes, who in turn had helped *him* escape the marshes—I didn't understand why he would return to England. He comes back, knowing the risk of being tossed into prison again just to see how his project of turning Pip into a gentleman has progressed; then it's up to

Pip and his new friend Herbert Pocket to help Magwitch escape a second time. I liked that. I could see the pattern.

"Curiosity killed the cat," was Mr. Watts' explanation. "If everything we did made sense, the world would be a different place. Life would be less interesting, don't you think?"

So Mr. Watts didn't really know either. When Mr. Watts read those final chapters I wasn't sure I had listened properly. If what I heard was correct, then it was unsatisfactory. Magwitch, it turns out, is Estella's father. Why had it taken so long to find out this fact? Our class had sat through fifty-nine days of readings, and what we now saw was a spider's web. Bits of story finding and connecting with one another. But what if the pattern I thought I was hearing was all wrong?

I would have to wait for the right moment to ask my questions. I didn't want to appear dumb. The book's magic hold on me was no secret, and often Mr. Watts singled me out to discuss something to do with the story. So, rather than shatter that confidence in me, I kept my mouth shut.

For several days after the final reading of *Great Expectations* our class felt flat. There was nothing to look forward to anymore. The story was at an end. So was our journeying in that world. We were back to our own. Without any prospect of escape, our days lost their purpose. We waited for Mr. Watts to come up with something new to fill that hole in our lives.

His solution, no doubt spurred by the rows of glum

faces, was to read *Great Expectations* a second time. Only this time we would share the task of reading it aloud. He thought it would be good for our English. Maybe. But nothing would change for our reading it a second time. The story was set. Pip would disappoint Joe Gargery, but Joe being Joe would find it in his heart to forgive. Pip would also chase after Estella—a rotten choice, but one he was committed to forever. Reading it a second or third or fourth time, as we did, would not change those events. Our only consolation was that by reading it a second and third time we would still have another country to flee to. And that would save our sanity.

We watched Mr. Watts walk to the desk and pick up his book. We waited to be chosen to begin the reading. As Mr. Watts turned around to face us, the book open at the graveyard scene, Daniel stuck up his hand.

"Yes, Daniel?" said Mr. Watts.

"What's it like to be white?"

Daniel immediately turned in his desk to look in my direction. Mr. Watts followed the trail, and chose to drop his gaze just short of my desk. So he knew where the question had come from. I knew he knew. Nevertheless he addressed his answer to Daniel.

"What is it like to be white? What is it like to be white on this island? A bit of what the last mammoth must have felt, I suppose. Lonely at times."

Mammoth? We had no idea what he meant. Even though Daniel's question was of great interest, we pretended we didn't care. We didn't want any part of that ambush, so we kept our follow-up questions to ourselves. Mr. Watts, though, had one of his own.

"What's it like to be black?"

He'd asked it of Daniel but now he looked at the whole class.

"Normal," said Daniel, for all of us.

I thought Mr. Watts was about to laugh. Maybe he was about to, before changing his mind and dropping his face into *Great Expectations*.

"I see," he said.

We got a better answer to Daniel's question a week later when the redskins came back to our village.

They arrived before dawn. Their helicopters put down way up the beach by the point and this side of the river. So we didn't have the same warning as last time. This time we were woken by voices and high whistles.

We had been waiting for this moment. Crazy as this may sound, we had willed it.

There are days when the humidity rises and rises and gets heavier and heavier until, at last, it bursts. The rain falls and you breathe again. That was how the tension of the past few weeks had felt. This is what happens, you wait and wait. Until you wish the redskins would just come so that the waiting can be over with.

It felt like something we had rehearsed, the way we came out of our houses. It was funny how we seemed to know what to do without being told or asked. The redskins had painted their faces black. We saw their eyes shift.

There was no shouting. There was no need. Everyone knew what to do. The soldiers and us. We were already known to one another.

When the redskin in charge spoke we were glad to hear it was a pleasant voice; we were expecting him to shout at us. What he wanted was simple enough. He wanted the names of everyone in our village. He said it was for security reasons, and we mustn't be afraid. He asked for our cooperation. We should give our names and our ages. He never once raised his voice. What he asked for was a simple thing to comply with—our names were not dangerous in any way: they were not explosives, they did not contain hidden fishhooks.

Two soldiers walked along our line taking down our names. In one or two cases we took the pen from the soldier to write our name correctly. We smiled as we did so. We were happy to help, especially with the correct spelling. The names did not take long to collect.

Two sheets of paper were handed to the officer. We watched him look slowly down the list. He was after a particular name, perhaps one from our village who had joined the rebels.

When the officer finally looked up it was clear he wasn't interested in us kids. He was only interested in grown-up faces. He took an interest in each one. Whenever one of our parents dropped their eyes he counted this as a victory. When he'd finished with staring down the last one he announced that he had a question. He said it wasn't a hard question and that all of us would know the answer. He smiled to himself when he said this. He asked why there were no young men in the village. There were girls, so why not young men?

He folded his arms and looked hard at the ground, as if sharing a curious puzzle with us. I felt he knew the answer but that wasn't really the point of the exercise. He wanted *us* to tell him. We also understood that to tell him what he already knew would be an admission of wrongdoing. We were being pecked at—the way a seabird will turn over a morsel of crab with its beak. He had all the information at his fingertips. But it wasn't enough. He wanted more.

For the moment we were saved from giving an answer. A soldier came jogging in from the beach. He spoke with the officer. We were too far away to hear what was said, but we saw the effect of the news on the officer—the wince at the corner of his mouth, the way his hand slapped his thigh. We watched him walk with the soldier in the direction of the beach. In a few minutes he came striding back. His light taunting mood of earlier was gone.

He walked along our line staring into our faces. When he got to the end he came and stood in front of us, clenched his hands behind his back, and rocked on his feet.

"Who is Pip?" he asked.

No one answered.

"I asked for all your names," he said. "You did not give me them all. Why?"

Those of us in Mr. Watts' class knew the answer. And my mum. But she had closed her eyes and ears. I thought she was praying. So she didn't see us kids catch one another's eye. Or the one beaming with the answer.

"Pip belongs to Mr. Dickens, sir," Daniel blurted out.

The officer walked over to where Daniel stood. "Who is this *Mis*ter Dickens?" he sneered.

And Daniel, who looked so proud to be giving the answers, pointed in the direction of the schoolhouse. We all knew where he meant; it wasn't the schoolhouse but the old church mission buried out of view by the vegetation.

The officer said something in pidgin to a number of his men. As one they looked off to where Daniel had pointed. The officer hadn't forgotten him. He snapped his fingers for Daniel to leave the line. He jogged into position as he had seen the soldiers do. The officer gave him a queer look. I thought he might hit Daniel for being insolent. Instead he placed a hand on Daniel's shoulder and instructed him to go with the soldiers to fetch this Mr. Dickens.

We were used to Mr. Watts in his suit. We were used to his eyes that wanted to leave his face, and the lean skinny frame that his clothes hung off. We had forgotten the shock of white in our sweating green world. And this we experienced all over again when Mr. Watts and his wife were rounded up by the soldiers.

The officer stood with his back to us, and as the parade approached from the direction of the schoolhouse he folded his arms. Daniel led the way. He looked so proud. He marched, swinging his arms at his sides. Now I saw Mr. Watts through redskin eyes. I saw all those things we had grown used to fresh again. Mr. Watts towered over the soldiers. He blinked in the sun, even though the light was not that strong at this hour. But then I don't think his blinking had to do with the sunlight. I'd seen Mr. Watts do this whenever my mum said something directly insulting. On those occasions I thought he was fighting back hurt feelings.

I may have got that wrong, however, because when he arrived at the clearing I saw blinking was his way to avoid eye contact. He looked everywhere but at us, the people and faces he knew. If you wanted to be critical you might have said he looked like the important and self-regarding white men that my grandfather had become part of a human pyramid for; he looked like a man about to make a speech, who was simply waiting to be invited to step forward.

There were other, smaller changes too. It was a while since we had last seen him wear a tie. His left hand fidgeted with where it was tied around his throat. He had found a shirt that buttoned up. He wore shoes. He was dressed like someone going to catch a plane.

The redskin soldiers seemed to forget about us. They stared at Mr. Watts, isolating him with their stare. Once more we saw what a strange fish had washed up on our shore.

They must have seen whites before. In Moresby there are plenty of whites. In Lae and Rabaul too. For years, until the hostilities, the whites from Australia used to run and operate the mine. We used to see their helicopters and light planes. We saw their pleasure craft out to sea. And if I had been older at that time, then I would have noticed, as my mum did, that whenever our men returned from the white world they came back changed in some way.

The officer walked across to Mr. Watts. He positioned himself half a step closer than he needed to do and peered up at his face.

"You are Mister Dickens."

Now, there was an obvious response available to Mr. Watts at this point. I expected him to clear up the confusion over Pip without fuss. Even Grace might have said something. But, as with my mum, she had closed her eyes, shut herself down to the point where she was physically present but otherwise not there.

Whatever Mr. Watts might have said changed the moment his eyes rested on Daniel, beaming, a step behind the officer. I think that's when he realized where the misunderstanding had come from, and a whole different set of circumstances resulted in Mr. Watts saying, "Yes, I am that man."

That was a lie that any one of us kids could have put right, and I understood, we all must have, the tremendous trust he placed in us at that moment. Daniel was the only one unaware of what was at stake. Either he didn't understand or simply failed to hear Mr. Watts step lightly into the skin of the greatest English author of the nineteenth century.

Here also was my mum's chance to squash her enemy, but she said nothing. Her eyes remained closed. The adults who could have corrected the situation were afraid of being singled out. A distance had opened up between us and Mr. Watts, between his whiteness and our blackness, and none of us wanted to have to stand next to where Mr. Watts stood all alone.

"Where is Mister Pip?" asked the officer.

Another white might have laughed out loud, but Mr. Watts showed the question respect.

"Sir, if I may explain. Pip is a creation. He is a character in a book."

The officer looked angry. The interrogation was drifting away from his control. He would have to ask what character, which book, and thereby reveal his ignorance. I could see those questions brewing in his face.

"I understand the confusion," Mr. Watts said at last. "If you allow me to, sir, I can show you the book and you will see that Pip is a character out of *Great Expectations*."

For the first time Mr. Watts looked to where the rest of us were. He singled me out. "Would you, Matilda? The book is on the desk."

I didn't move until the officer gave a quick nod.

I thought he would pick a soldier to go with me but he didn't. One soldier, his weapon cradled in his arm, turned to watch me run to the schoolhouse. For the short distance I had to go I did not forget those bloodshot eyes or his gun. I knew what I had to do. I had to carry out the task as quickly and faithfully as possible.

I ran into the empty classroom and stopped. *Great*

Expectations was not where Mr. Watts had said it was. I walked up the aisles. I looked over the desktops. I crouched down to see if it had fallen on the floor. I looked up at the ceiling. The family of pale geckos was stock-still from when my rushing feet entered the room. Their black eyes, which watched me on so many other occasions, were flat and blank. Those lizards would not help even if they knew where the book was.

Now I knew fear as Pip had known it when Magwitch threatened to tear his heart and liver out if he didn't return in the morning with food and a file. I felt singled out by this darkness that had descended over our lives. As I left the schoolhouse I saw all the village, the soldiers, the officer, and Mr. Watts looking in my direction. I ran past the soldier with the bloodshot eyes. I did not speak to the officer. I ran up to Mr. Watts. I almost made the mistake of addressing him as Mr. Watts.

"The book is not there, sir," I said.

If ever there was a time for Mr. Watts to show his fear, this would have been it.

"Are you sure, Matilda?"

"It is not on the desk, sir."

Mr. Watts looked mildly surprised. He gazed off into the nearby trees while he considered where the book might be.

The officer glowered at me.

"There is no book?"

"There is a book, sir. I cannot find it."

"No. I have been lied to. There is no book."

The officer shouted out an order to his men to search every house. Mr. Watts tried to say something but the redskin cut him short. He jabbed his finger at Mr. Watts' chest.

"No! You stay here. All of you stay here."

He chose two soldiers to watch over us with their weapons, then joined his men in their search for Pip.

We watched them enter our houses. We heard them breaking up our things. They began to pull things out of our houses. Our sleeping mats. Our clothes. The few possessions we had. They put everything in a big heap. When they had done that the officer gave an order to the two men watching over us. They were to march us over to the pile.

There was a dangerous new look in the officer's face. The earlier anger was gone. In its place was a cold and calculating look. One way or another he would end up on top. He would make us pay for our lack of cooperation.

Once we were reassembled (and our number now included Mr. Watts and Grace) he lit a match. He held it up so we could all see.

"I will give you one more chance. Bring me this man Pip or I will burn your possessions."

None of us said anything. We looked at the ground. This is when I heard Mr. Watts clear his throat. I knew that gesture, so did the others, and we looked up to see Mr. Watts advance towards the officer.

"If I can explain, sir. The man you are looking for is a

fiction, a made-up character. He is out of a novel . . ." And here he would customarily have said *by the greatest English author of the nineteenth century. His name is Charles Dickens.* But another thought caught, and I saw it register in his face, perhaps just in time, that Daniel had already revealed him to be Mr. Dickens. He had taken that identity to protect Daniel. He might make things worse if he now said he wasn't Mr. Dickens.

For the first time Mr. Watts looked worried. What could he say further to make the redskin officer understand? The truth would only make the officer look foolish in front of his men. All these different aspects of the problem revealed themselves in Mr. Watts' face. And now the redskin mistook Mr. Watts' hesitation for a lack of conviction.

"Why should I believe you? You asked me to believe this man is in a book. When I ask for the book there is no book."

That was something Mr. Watts could defend, but when he opened his mouth to say something the officer held up a hand to silence him.

"No. You will speak to me when I ask you to. I am not interested in any more of your lies."

He turned to face the rest of us.

"You people are concealing a man known by the name of Pip. I give you one last chance to hand this man over. If you do not, I will suspect you of concealing a rebel. This is your last chance. Now, give me this man."

We would have handed over Pip were it possible, but we could not hand over what we didn't possess—at least in the sense that the redskin officer understood.

He struck a second match and held it up for all to see. This time, no one looked at the ground. We watched the flame burn down to his fingers. Daniel saw something of his sticking out of the pile. He casually began to walk over. He intended to pick out a plastic ball, as if someone had made a stupid mistake by placing it there in the first place. That's what he had in mind to do when a soldier blocked him with his rifle and walked him backwards to our line.

I looked over at my mum. She pretended to have a splinter in her palm. She shook her hand and muttered to herself. She bent over, held her wrist up close to her face, and studied an injury only she could see.

The officer shouted an order. Two soldiers emptied kerosene over our sleeping mats and clothes. The officer struck another match and threw it on the pile. A flame burst up and licked across the trail of fuel. The fire was only skin-deep at this point. Now it began to smoke. Seconds later the pile burst into a bigger flame. Our things spit and spat like pork fat. It took no longer than five minutes to incinerate all our belongings. We were left with only the clothes we stood in.

The officer didn't look happy, or vengeful. He looked like a man sadly resigned to conducting such business.

He dropped at the shoulders. He appeared to sink inside himself, perhaps to a darker place. Everything had just got much more serious. In the sort of solemn voice I had last heard from the minister, he announced, "You have been foolish. You cannot defeat me with your lies. I will give you two weeks to think about your decision. Next time we come here I expect this man Pip to be handed over."

The officer looked us over one last time, then made his way back to the beach. His soldiers followed like a pack of dogs after their master.

FOR A WHILE WE STOOD AROUND THE charred embers. No one saying anything. I may have heard a woman sniff back tears over something she'd lost to the flames. Gilbert's dad used a stick to poke around until he found a fishing reel. He dragged it away. It was made of plastic, which had partly melted away. That was the state of most of our things. A trace of their original condition remained, but they were damaged beyond use. Of our sleeping mats there was not a shred left.

There were people without kids who did not know about *Great Expectations*. These grown-ups had no idea who Pip was or what the fuss was about. They assumed it was a matter of mistaken identity. Or that the person wanted by the redskins was living further up the coast. I heard that rumor, and even some smug statements concerning that person's whereabouts. But those with kids in Mr. Watts' class knew where to place the blame for their misfortune. And these were the people who Mr. Watts addressed in a voice more sad and regretful than I'd ever heard him use, apart from the time he read chapter 56 of

Great Expectations, where Magwitch, recaptured, lies in prison, a sick old man awaiting trial. Mr. Watts' tone had left no doubt about whom we should pity.

Now he had the impossible job of accepting responsibility for the fire and the lost possessions of the village. People were still prodding the gray smoking coals in the wild hope of recovering something as small as a hair clip, when Mr. Watts walked slowly towards the smoldering remains. It was one of those moments that no one needs to explain, where people slip easily into the roles of the aggrieved. Mr. Watts didn't try to duck the blame. But his apology had an unexpected starting point, and later I wondered if he designed it that way to defuse any anger he suspected might come his way.

"Yesterday marked the tenth anniversary since Grace and I first moved here. We have had so many memories, so many wonderful experiences. I don't know how we arrived at the events of today. I don't know what I can tell you or say, because no words can replace the things you have lost. But please believe me when I say Pip is a confusion that I failed to see coming until it was too late. I am so sorry."

Those he spoke to couldn't meet his eye. Those who did, my mum included, let the white man bake in the hot sun without the courtesy of a reply.

Some took themselves off to their empty houses. Some chose to rake the embers—in case something had been missed. In one or two cases people could be seen smiling over something they held in their hand. Others, with machetes, went off to the jungle to cut down spear leaves for new sleeping mats.

Mr. Watts waited for a reply, any reply, but there was none. It was left to Grace to take hold of his wrist and turn him back to the old mission house. I watched them walk away, one white and skinny, the other black and heavy in the hip.

I wanted to run after them and say something that would make it better for Mr. Watts. I wanted to, but I did nothing.

Instead I went into our house to see if the soldiers had overlooked anything. They had. Wedged into a corner was the pencil I used to keep my calendar. And up on one of the rafters was my father's sleeping mat. I don't imagine the soldiers had spared it for any reason other than their failure to see it. My mum would be pleased. It would be something at least, and it was the only thing she had left to remind her of my father. I thought I would spread it over the floor. It would be a nice surprise for her.

As I pulled the mat down I felt something hard and small about the size of a river stone. And even as I was thinking *stone* my thoughts leaped onto another possibility. I quickly unrolled the mat and there was Mr. Watts' copy of *Great Expectations*.

It is hard to put into words my feelings of betrayal at that moment.

I thought back to my mum standing in our frightened line, her eyes closed. What had her ears been doing? Had she not heard the redskin officer ask for the book—not once, but many times? And what were her eyes and ears doing when the same redskin had stood with a match burning down to his fingers as he asked once more, then for a final time, for someone to produce either Pip or the book in which he was said to appear?

Even as I asked myself these questions I knew what she had been doing. Her silence was meant to destroy Pip and the standing of Mr. Watts, a godless white man who would seek to place in her daughter's head a make-believe person with the same status as her kin. She had kept silent when she could have saved the possessions of the village.

But now I saw her problem, because it was also my problem. If she had run back to our house to produce the book she would have had to explain how it got there in the first place. For the same reason, I could not give the book back to Mr. Watts. I would have to say where I had found it. To do so would be to betray my mum. She was stuck, and now I was stuck too. I had no choice but to roll the mat back up with that dog-eared copy of *Great Expectations* inside, and stick it back up on the rafters for my mother to find.

⁂

WE FOUND WAYS to console ourselves. We reminded ourselves of what we still had. The fish were still in the sea. The fruits were still in the trees. The redskin soldiers had left us the air and shade.

If I was my mum I might have asked myself, *What use is all that to me if I have lost my daughter?* Immediately after the redskins left she was nowhere to be found. I didn't look too hard, but later, when I saw her down the beach, I was happy just to locate her.

I didn't need to go near her. I couldn't bear that. Part of me, though, wanted her to know that I knew what she had done. I wanted her to know that I knew.

Later that night, when we tried to make ourselves comfortable on the floorboards—she pretended not to notice my father's sleeping mat—she wrapped herself up in a thick silence. Obviously she did not want to talk about the redskin soldiers. Our house must have been the only one not to have that conversation. As soon as she lay down she turned her head away from me. I don't think either one of us slept.

In the morning, to escape the suffocating air of guilt, I went down to the beach, and there I discovered my shrine to Pip was destroyed. The shells and heart seeds had been kicked away. After the trouble the first one caused I had no wish to create another PIP in the sand.

We had lost things, irreplaceable things such as my father's postcards. I remember one with a picture of a parrot. Another featured a kangaroo. There were my father's clothes, which my mum used to keep folded together in a corner, as if he might stroll back into our lives at any moment. Once I found her holding my father's shirt to her face. Well, all that was gone, along with my sneakers. They had arrived in the last package before the blockade. I didn't wear them because they made my feet hurt. When I wondered why my father had sent me the wrong size I realized

I was a smaller person in his memory than I was now. They were useless but I couldn't give them away; I couldn't give them away because they were from my father.

Our few photographs also ended up in the fire, including the only ones of my dad taken on the island. The photos are gone, but I still remember them. One had him sitting with my mum at the fishermen's club in Kieta at a Christmas work function. In the photograph my mum is much younger. She has a flower tucked behind her ear. Her bottom lip has dropped like a bud opening to welcome the smile onto her face. My dad has his arm around her. They lean forward as if interested in the question from their daughter holding this photograph years later: *How did you achieve such happiness? And what happened to it?*

You would never guess that a hairbrush and a toothbrush could be so important and necessary. You don't think a plate or a bowl is important until you don't have either. On the other hand, you never knew a single coconut could have so many uses.

There was one curious outcome in all of this. My mum's silence meant that while Mr. Watts' copy of *Great Expectations* was saved, her beloved pidgin Bible went on the bonfire.

PEOPLE AVOIDED MR. WATTS for days. Groups either drew in closer, like a clump of bananas, or dispersed whenever he came near. Mr. Watts did not chase after them. He wasn't interested in pleading his blamelessness. You might almost have thought he failed to notice the coolness of everyone; but I knew Mr. Watts better than that. As I had come to know the meaning of *mammoth,* I would have said that Mr. Watts felt as lonely as the last mammoth.

People turned their minds back to the matter of Pip. By now, everyone in the village knew about him or thought they did, and some hotheads now mounted their own searches. I stood with my mum in our separate silence as groups of silly men armed with machetes disappeared into the jungle to hunt him down.

Others who knew about the book and Pip's place in it wondered where the book might be. The redskin soldiers would be back and the one thing that would save their houses would be to find that book with the name of Pip scattered across its pages. My mum must have known this. I imagine this very thing weighed on her conscience. She must have thought about hiding the book outside somewhere so it might be found.

She was not a stupid woman. She must have considered her options whenever she heard a fearful neighbor speculate on when the redskins would come back. And when the night sunk in around us, long and dense, she must have lain awake thinking—knowing what the right thing to do was, but also wondering if there was another way. Once, she might have said something to me. She might have confessed and asked for my help or just my ears. But I was too far away for her to confide in or to ask for my opinion. Even though I lay next to her, in the dark my silence placed me at a distance she could not reach. Of all the people she could not bear to disappoint, I was top of that list. Her daughter who resented her, not only for what our neighbors had lost but for the blame placed at Mr. Watts' door. If I had been willing or able to break my silence I would have thrown her own language back at her. I would have said the devil had gotten into her.

AT NIGHT WE LISTENED TO GUNFIRE. There were no battles. This was the loose gunfire of rambos drunk on jungle juice trying to scare the redskins. They took aim at the stars and blasted up through the treetops. But there were also other nights of gunfire where stems of smoke greeted the dawn and we knew we were seeing the aftermath of something we did not want to send our minds to.

We were back to waiting for the redskin soldiers, and like before, the tension rose. People squabbled. Voices were raised. Wives fought with their husbands, and vice versa. Kids were shouted at. You saw little kids squirt across yards where we used to see roosters.

And one morning we saw Mr. Watts pull his wife, Grace, along in that trolley. For the occasion Mr. Watts had put on his red clown's nose. He was back to being Pop Eye, and that came as a shock—to see him slip once more into that role, but also to see how quickly we changed back to our old idea of him.

When people saw him pulling Grace along it dawned on

them, as a mob, that the Wattses' house had been spared. Mr. Watts and Grace must still have their possessions. The proof was that stupid red clown's nose and the cart. No one could remember seeing their things dragged to the bonfire. But then no one would have expected it either because Mr. Watts was white and therefore lived outside the world in which these things happened.

It then occurred to people that Mr. Watts might have the missing book that would save their houses.

I did not join the rush on Mr. Watts and Grace's house. Of course not. I did not want Mr. Watts to look up and see his Matilda as part of that mob. Besides, I knew their search was a waste of time. *Great Expectations* was rolled up in my father's sleeping mat hanging from the rafter above the floor where my mum slept. Never in my life, not up to that moment or since, really, have I held such valuable information.

Now I knew something of the moral confusion my mum had experienced. As my neighbors rushed towards Mr. Watts' house I had the information that could have stopped them, but I said nothing, and did nothing.

Here is how a coward thinks: *If I stay inside my house I won't have to witness the ransacking of the Wattses' house. I won't have to know.*

I don't know whether they looked for the book at the house, then, after searching far and wide for it, fell to anger and frustration. There was no way of knowing the precise nature of the mood of the mob.

But when I moved to the edge of the door and looked

out I saw people carrying all the possessions belonging to the Wattses. Nothing was too small. Useless appliances with cords and plugs bouncing behind in the dirt. One woman carried a plastic clothes basket. She looked like she might be interested in hanging on to that for herself. But no one took things for themselves. They dragged the larger items. Men carried some of the furniture between them like a pig about to be spit-roast. I counted one or two smiles. But, I'm glad to say, I heard no cheering.

I had never seen an event like this before; I had never seen anything as vengeful as this, and yet, once again, the people went about it as if they knew what to do. No one had to tell them where to put everything. And they had many, many things. Stuff that was of value to us, but no one took anything. There were clothes. Photographs. Chairs. Ornaments made of wood. Carvings. A small table. And books. I had never seen so many books—I thought Mr. Watts might have given them to us kids to read.

Everything went up in flames.

This bonfire was more spectacular than the last. There was more wood. We watched the flames in silence. No one tried to hide their involvement, nor did the Wattses try to put out the blaze. There were no words of anger or blame.

Mr. Watts stood before the blaze with one arm around the shoulders of Grace. They looked as if they were farewelling someone. If he stopped short of appearing as a participant, Mr. Watts made what was happening seem necessary and acceptable.

*

THIS TIME WHEN the redskins reappeared it was as if they melted out of the jungle. They came upon us like cats. The last one out of the jungle was their commanding officer.

Some of the soldiers wore bandages that had bloodstains on them. Some of the bandages were strips torn from their shirts. Their officer looked to be sick with fever. His skin was jaundiced. The eyes of his men were inflamed and red, whereas his were yellow. Sweat coated his face; it oozed from him. He seemed too tired and ill for anger.

Once more we gathered without an order to do so. Some of the soldiers wandered off on their own, their weapons swinging lightly from their shoulders. I saw one enter a house and undo his trousers to urinate.

We all looked back at the officer. Surely he would have something to say about this—one of his men urinating in our houses? But he either didn't want to know or didn't care. When he spoke he sounded tired; that's when I noticed he was having trouble standing. He was very sick.

He told us he wanted food and medicines. Mabel's father held up his hand to speak on our behalf. "We have no medicines," he said. This was true. It was also bad news. Very bad news. The bonfire must have slipped the officer's memory, because now we saw the reason why we had no medicines dawn on his sick face.

He rolled his head back on his shoulders and gazed up

at the blue sky. He didn't have a reason to be annoyed with us. Mabel's father had given the information politely and without mention of the bonfire. All the same, the news appeared to deflate the officer. He was tired of being who he was: tired of his job, tired of this island, of us, and of the responsibility he carried.

One of his men brought him a pineapple. Perhaps it was to cheer him up. The soldier held it in both hands as an offering. The officer acknowledged the pineapple with a nod, but he waved it away. When he raised his fevered eyes we knew what was coming next.

"Last time we were here you concealed a man from us. You saw what happened because of your foolishness. I decided to give you time to think about your decision. That is why we went away. To give you time to think. Now we are back with our request."

My mum closed her eyes, and this time I followed her example. So the next part I only heard. "I must warn you all," I heard the officer say, "I do not have the patience that I had when you last saw me."

There was a pause. As it lengthened I felt the thick heat of the midday sun. I heard the too joyful screech of a crow. Then I heard the redskin say, "Bring me this man Pip."

There were people who might have spoken up. Mr. Watts, for one, had he been there. The soldiers must have forgotten where to find his house. Either that or they chose not to. I knew Grace had come down with fever, and I understood Mr. Watts was nursing her as best he could.

The other person who could have saved us was my

mum. But she could not produce the book, not after the bonfire, which happened because of her failure to produce the book the first time. She couldn't do that, any more than I could betray her and lead the soldiers to my father's sleeping mat.

Under these circumstances, silence among such a large group of people is an uncomfortable thing to experience. Guilt spreads around even to those who have nothing to feel guilty about. Many held their breath. Or, as I heard later, many did what me and my mum did and closed their eyes. We closed our eyes in a bid to remove ourselves.

I remember hearing a wave slap playfully onto the beach. It had not occurred to me before to think of the ocean as a dumb useless thing.

"Very well," said the officer without enthusiasm. It was almost possible to imagine that he wished he hadn't said that. It was almost possible to think that we had forced him to act, that we had given him no choice. That *we* were the ones to blame for everything.

I will say this for the soldiers. They went about burning our houses with appropriate solemnity. There were no wild shouts of joy. They didn't let off rounds of ammunition. It wasn't what you might expect. No. They asked us to burn our homes. They splashed kerosene in the doorway, then stepped back for the owner of the house to throw a lit torch in the doorway. My mother did so knowing that Mr. Watts' copy of *Great Expectations* would be lost forever.

As we watched the flames devour our houses it was like saying good-bye to a part of our lives. We missed that space. We hadn't thought of it in that way until then. Now some of us had an idea of what Mr. Watts had given up. People shut their eyes and recalled smells of meals eaten, old scents, conversations—some arguments, but also perhaps important decisions—celebrations, all of which had happened under a roof. Some of our neighbors spoke of a quiet stillness. Things you would have thought could be found elsewhere. There is stillness out to sea and under tall trees as well, but I suppose they didn't know about this other quality of stillness until their houses were destroyed.

In the first fire people had lost gifts and favorite things. A ball. A lucky fishhook. In my case, the shoes my father had sent me. The postcards. This time what people lost was their privacy. Where would they hide themselves now? I shared that same concern.

I had discovered that the plainest house can crown a fantasy or daydream. An open window can be tolerated. So can an open door. But I discovered the value of four walls and a roof. Something about containment that at the same time offers escape.

I worried about my secret life with Pip. Would I find him again under the trees or along the beach? I worried that the world around me would speak too loudly and want my company too much.

We slept outside the smoking ruins of our houses. We discovered that without a house your life feels bare. We had only the clothes we slept in. Yet some things cannot be taken or set fire to or shot. We still had the air. We still had the freshwater streams. We had fruit. We had our gardens.

We were even left our pigs. And, by some stroke of good fortune, the redskin soldiers had also overlooked Gilbert's father's boat. It was up the dry creek bed where he always hauled it. When I saw its blue hull tipped over on its keel I felt a fish leap in my heart. We pounced on his nets and fishing tackle like the gifts they were. These were small, important victories in our bid to survive.

Gilbert's father suddenly looked like a man who had just awoken to his responsibilities. He was an expert fisherman who knew where to set his nets and where to find fish at night. He had been born with this fish sense. He knew fish better than the fish knew themselves, which was just as well because night was the only time he could risk fishing. If the redskin patrols saw his boat they would shoot on sight. We knew this because we had heard of such events happening further up the coast.

After two days the smoldering stopped, and we saw there was nothing left. Soon you could hear the chop-chop of machetes. People came and went out of the jungle. They carried spear leaves and long stripped branches. Two men could carry a heavy beam between them.

Within a week we had built new houses. These were not as good as our old ones. We didn't have milled timber or wooden floors. But they were as good as we could make with what we had. We stitched and wove them together. Everyone has seen a bird build its nest—well, that was us too.

The classroom block was one of only two buildings left standing. That was odd. My mum thought it was because the block was government property. It made no sense for the redskins to destroy it. It would be like destroying a bit of Moresby. The other place was Mr. Watts' house. Again, my mum thought she knew why, saying it was because Mr. Watts was white. The redskins wouldn't do anything to cause white displeasure. Port Moresby was dependent on Australian aid, which came in many forms—teachers, missionaries, canned fish, and even the helicopters used to drop the rebels out to sea.

This time no one rushed to set fire to Mr. Watts' house. People knew about Grace's fever, but it wasn't just that. I think they learned from the first time, after throwing Mr. Watts' things onto the fire, that it didn't make them feel any better.

Possibly this also explains why no one stopped their kids from attending Mr. Watts' class.

But there was one change. Our class was only half the size it had been. Some of the older boys had run off to join the rebels. And one girl, Genevieve, who was probably the one least interested in school and *Great Expectations,* had joined her brothers and sisters to walk to their relatives' village up in the hills.

MR. WATTS BEGAN BY THANKING US FOR turning up. He had been unsure whether he would make it himself. Mrs. Watts was very sick. But here he was, and here we were, almost like old times, he might have said. Except what we had lost and what we had taken from Mr. Watts and his wife came between us in small but telling ways. We found ourselves looking away rather than meeting Mr. Watts' eyes. And his own steady gaze sought the corners of the ceiling at the far end of the room. We slipped under that gaze and watched what he did with his hands. We prepared ourselves to listen out for any hard-done-by note to slip into his voice.

"We have all lost our possessions and many of us our homes," he said. "But these losses, severe though they may seem, remind us of what no person can take, and that is our minds and our imaginations."

Daniel stuck up his hand.

"Yes, Daniel?"

"Where are our imaginations?"

"Out there, Daniel."

We all turned to see what Mr. Watts was pointing to out the door.

"And in here."

Our heads switched back to see him tap the side of his head.

"Close your eyes," he said to Daniel, "and in a voice only you can hear, say your name. Say it to yourself only."

I had moved to a desk two behind Daniel, so I could see the sides of his cheeks move with the spoken sound of his name.

"Have you found it, Daniel?"

"Yes, Mr. Watts. I have."

"Let's all do it," said Mr. Watts. "Close your eyes and silently recite your name."

The sound of my name took me to a place deep inside my head. I already knew that words could take you into a new world, but I didn't know that on the strength of one word spoken for my ears only I would find myself in a room that no one else knew about. Matilda. Matilda. Matilda. I said it over and over. I tried out different versions, dragging the word out and expanding that room. *Ma til da*.

"Another thing," Mr. Watts said. "No one in the history of your short lives has used the same voice as you with which to say your name. This is yours. Your special gift that no one can ever take from you. This is what our friend and colleague Mr. Dickens used to construct his stories with."

Mr. Watts stopped to look, checking to see if he was traveling too fast for us and whether what he had said had sunk in.

I replied with a nod and Mr. Watts continued.

"Now, when Mr. Dickens sat down in 1860 to write *Great Expectations,* the first thing he did was clear a space for Pip's voice. That is what we did. We located that little room in ourselves where our voice is pure and alive. Mr. Dickens closed his eyes and waited until he heard that first line."

Mr. Watts closed his eyes and we waited. He must have thought this was something he could test us with, because he snapped open his eyes to ask if anyone remembered that first line. None of us did. So he remembered for us. And as he closed his eyes a second time he quoted a line which is now ingrained in me as much as my own name. I will take to the grave the words Mr. Watts recited to us kids: *My father's family name being Pirrip, and my Christian name Philip, my infant tongue could make of both names nothing longer or more explicit than Pip. So I called myself Pip, and came to be called Pip.*

At another time, all this talk of rooms and voices might have confused us. But the loss of our houses helped us to understand that what they had kept safe was more than our possessions; our houses had concealed our selves that no one else ever saw when we lay on our sleeping mats at night. Now Mr. Watts had given us all another room to lounge around in. The next stage was to furnish it.

To that end Mr. Watts announced a special task. We would retrieve *Great Expectations.*

Some of us were not sure what Mr. Watts meant by the word *retrieve*. Then when it became clear—thanks to Daniel's question—we still wondered if we understood. *Great Expectations* had gone up in flames and could not be retrieved from the ashes. Of course Mr. Watts had a different approach in mind. "Let's see if we can remember it," he said.

And that's what we did; not in an hour but over many weeks, more likely it was months. After my pencil and calendar were lost in the burning of our houses, I didn't bother with recording the passing of time. One day blended into the next.

Mr. Watts instructed us to dream freely. We did not have to remember the story in any order or even as it really happened, but as it came to us. "You won't always remember at a convenient moment," he warned us. "It might come to you in the night. If so, you must hang on to that fragment until we meet in class. There you can share it, and add it to the others. When we have gathered all the fragments we will put together the story. It will be as good as new."

We had done this sort of thing before. In the past, when we still had our nets and lines, we would divide up the catch on the beach. That's what we set out to do now with *Great Expectations*.

In the class that day we did not retrieve much. It was

hard to hold a thought steady. You only had to look out the door to see a scrub fowl wander into view, or stare ahead to consider the white whiskers emerging in Mr. Watts' beard. A stray thought like that could hook you. There was nothing left in the world to think about after remembering the taste of scrub fowl or wondering about Mr. Watts getting older so quickly.

Once I began to turn up fragments of *Great Expectations* it was surprising where and when I found them. This was most often at night, when I needed another world to escape to, but it also would occur in unexpected moments. I might be gazing out to sea thinking of nothing in particular, and then, without warning, I would find myself with Pip walking up to Satis House with its cobwebs and gloom, and its determination to look backwards.

I remembered how I felt, how protective I had been towards Pip. I didn't like the way Estella spoke to him, and I didn't like the way Sarah Pocket teased and taunted him with gossip. I could never understand why Pip would accept the baiting of those two and never spat back.

There. I had two fragments. The first—Miss Havisham's decision to stop the clocks—I took to class. I was so terrified I would forget it, I didn't allow myself to be spoken to. I turned my head away from the other kids rather than risk having my fragment make room for other thoughts and conversations. I had it stored in the little room as Mr. Watts had directed us to. I had closed the door. But I didn't know how secure that door was, or what would happen once other people's voices started pounding on it.

Around this time Mr. Watts shared a secret with us kids. It came after Celia shared her fragment—the scene when Pip comes home from giving his sister's pie to Magwitch and finds the armed constabulary in the kitchen. Celia claimed to know Pip's heart of guilt. Yet she wondered how she had come to think the police were there to arrest Pip. Where had that come from? she asked aloud. How was it that she had conjured up something that was not in the book?

I had always liked her, but now I admired Celia. I hadn't stopped to think that someone else might also treasure the book and actively inhabit that world. The quality of Celia's question meant that the book must also occupy her thoughts. Possibly Pip too.

Mr. Watts thanked Celia. Her comment, he said, provided us with an interesting insight into the parallel world the reader develops from the words on the page. "Thank you, thank you," he said, and Celia glowed in this praise.

Mr. Watts put it to the rest of the class. "What shall we do with Celia's fragment? How can we save it to make sure we don't forget it?"

We wondered aloud. Our hands shot up with suggestions. We could find a stick and write it down in the sand—Daniel's idea. We fell silent. Gilbert raised his hand. We could write it in a secret place. Mr. Watts liked that idea. He stuck up his finger so our minds could group around Gilbert's recommendation.

"A secret place is a fine idea. But it would have to be *completely* safe," warned Mr. Watts.

We agreed.

"It would have to be *our* secret." There was no doubting where his emphasis lay. He looked around at our faces, and we saw his seriousness. I thought there must be some danger associated with this secret, whatever it was. "Our secret," he said once more.

He reached inside the breast pocket of his jacket and took out an exercise book. It had been folded in half to fit his pocket. Mr. Watts smoothed it out on his desk, then held it up for all of us kids to see. With his other hand he reached into another pocket to produce a pencil. Years later I would see on TV a magician produce a white rabbit with a similar flourish. It was a wonderful sight but not nearly as astonishing as what Mr. Watts produced. *Astonishing* is not too strong a word if you lived the way we did. Privately, though, each of us wondered how Mr. Watts had saved these items from the bonfire.

Mr. Watts smiled at our gaping faces. "What a responsibility we have," he said. "What a responsibility. We must make sure that Mr. Dickens' greatest book is not lost forever." He began to pace up and down the center aisle. "Can you imagine if it was lost forever? Just think. Future generations could point their finger at us and accuse us all of not looking after what we had been given to take care of."

We tried to look how we felt we should in this situation. Solemn. Serious.

"Right, then," he said. "I take your silence to be agreement. Entry number one is Celia's."

Mr. Watts returned to the desk, sat, and began to write. Once when he looked up we thought he had forgotten something and I saw Celia half rise from her chair. Mr. Watts resumed writing and she sat down again. When he finished he stared at what he had written. "I wonder if I've gotten everything down correctly," he said. "Let's find out." He read back the words. Celia blushed. It was clear Mr. Watts had added a line or two of his own. He looked up and found Celia. She gave him a quick nod and Mr. Watts pretended to look relieved.

Now he looked around for another contribution. "Matilda, what have you got for us?"

As I retrieved my scene with Pip making his way to Satis House, Mr. Watts smiled to himself, and before I had even finished he was bent over, scribbling in the exercise book.

When I started on my second fragment he stopped writing, raised his eyes, and looked away. He looked so troubled I lost all confidence. Perhaps I had failed to remember correctly.

"Estella's remorseless teasing of Pip," he said at last. "This is an important aspect of their relationship. He loves what he cannot have."

He stopped there and pushed back in his chair. His large eyes flicked up to the stunned geckos stuck over the ceiling. Then he stood up abruptly and walked to the door. He looked out at the brilliant green sunshine.

What did he find out there? Where did his thoughts go to? London? Australia? To his white tribe? Home?

We saw him nod again, as if he'd just found what it was he was after. He swung around to face us and his eyes went straight to my desk.

"We need words, Matilda. We need to remember what Estella actually says to Pip."

The others sitting in the front turned to look at me. Along with Mr. Watts they waited for me to retrieve the words. My mind went blank. I could not remember word for word what Estella had said to Pip, and as that became clear to the others, one by one their heads turned back to the front. We waited for Mr. Watts to walk back to the desk. He looked like a man made weary by bad news.

"I should warn you," he said, "this will be the hardest part of our task. But it is an important part. We must try hard to remember what one character says to another." As he said this he appeared overtaken by a separate thought. "However, if we can get the gist of what is meant, that will be something, at least."

Gist. This needed explaining. Mr. Watts put it this way. "If I say *tree,* I will think English oak, you will think palm tree. They are both trees. A palm and an oak both successfully describe what a tree is, but they are different trees."

So this is what *gist* meant. We could fill in the gaps with our own worlds. I saw Gilbert scratch his head before deciding to stick his hand up.

"What about the canoe tree?"

It was plain Mr. Watts wasn't sure what a canoe tree was.

"What's its other name, Gilbert?"

"Just canoe tree," he said.

Mr. Watts decided to gamble.

"A canoe tree qualifies."

Gilbert sat back pleased.

Gist examples were to be a matter of last resort. I knew what Mr. Watts was after. He wanted the actual words. But the more I tried to remember Estella's cruel words to Pip, the more they drifted away from me. The day world kept intruding and mocking my attempts at remembering.

*

MY MUM HAD PACKED away her guilt someplace and recovered her voice. And now, as if to make up for lost time, she returned to her favorite pastime of constant put-downs of Mr. Watts, or Pop Eye, as she was back to calling him.

Pop Eye. She put all her contempt into that name. Pop Eye is a man who stands beneath a coconut tree never believing a coconut will fall until it lands on his head. He would eat a sunfish, given half a chance. Dumb bugger. Does your Mr. Watts know a stonefish when he sees one? His ignorance makes him a dangerous man. And you, Matilda, why do you look to an ignorant, dangerous man for a teacher? This is how crazy the world has become. Can your Mr. Watts build a house? Can he paddle out to the reef at sunset and sneak up on a shoal of parrot fish?

Your Mr. Watts is dependent on other souls to feed him and his wife. He is nothing by himself.

Once upon a time I would have walked away from her attack on Mr. Watts—now I listened. In her mocking I could hear Estella. So I trailed after her like a mangy dog after a scrap of food. I followed her from our crude shelter to the garden to the creek until she tried to bat me away. She called me names. I was a mosquito. I was a tick on a dog's arse. "What's the matter with you, girl? Do you not have a shadow of your own to play with?"

Most of the time her words fell harmlessly off me. But that last sentence stuck. *Do you not have a shadow of your own to play with?* I smiled at my mum. I wanted to thank her, but I didn't know how. I went to hug her, but she saw that coming and took a step back. She raised her hands, pretending I had turned into a demon. I couldn't speak in case what she had said escaped my mouth with the other words. I was a bird with a worm caught in its beak.

I ran to Mr. Watts' house with my fragment. I wasn't going to let it leak from my mind. I ran past the schoolhouse and followed a path half covered in overgrowth. One of the more general criticisms directed Mr. Watts' way was that he didn't take care of his property. And it wasn't just my mum who said this. But as every other house was burned to the ground, I wonder if there was purpose behind Mr. Watts' neglect, that in the end he was the smart one.

As I made my way there I felt a bit like Pip approaching

Satis House. I also felt nervous. At least Pip had been invited by Miss Havisham. I hoped Mr. Watts wouldn't mind my turning up like this. I thought he wouldn't mind so much, given the responsibility of our task and once he heard the quality of my fragment.

The house came into view and I found myself stalled by the memories it stirred inside me. The sight of the wooden steps and wooden gables and door. These things were beautiful reminders of the outside world.

I climbed the steps to a small verandah and peered in the open door to a large room. On this side of the house the shutters were partially closed and the light cast a wide rippled path across the wooden floor. In the corner I could make out Mrs. Watts. She lay on her sleeping mat. Most of her was obscured by Mr. Watts. He knelt beside his sick wife, stroking her hair and dabbing her forehead with a damp-looking rag.

My eyes greedily took in a ceiling fan and a standing fan (neither working, of course). On a far bench I could see a large can of corned beef. I couldn't remember when I last saw such a can, any can for that matter. But whenever that was I'm sure I would never have been able to imagine a day in the future when an ordinary thing such as a can would represent a broad hope.

I put away the surprise of these things and stepped inside the room. I couldn't hold on to my fragment any longer. The doors flew open and I blurted—

"Do you not have a shadow of your own to play with?"

Mr. Watts slowly turned his head and at once I realized

my mistake in coming here. He wasn't as pleased to see me as I had hoped, nor did my fragment make the sort of impression I was expecting. He looked to me, to explain.

"It's gist," I said. "What Estella says to Pip."

I was used to Mr. Watts' silences and that way of his of walking to the open door of the classroom as if all the answers to everything lay outside, and where he stood on the brink of confirming our wild guesses as right or wrong according to what he could see.

So I waited and waited, and finally, with what seemed a huge effort, he stirred himself sufficiently to turn back into the teacher I knew, and said, "I think that gets to the heart of the matter, Matilda." He looked up at the ceiling for a moment. "Yes, I think so," he said.

Only now did I pay slight attention to the heaviness of his voice, but I did not see his sadness. I felt only the disappointment of his underwhelming response. His eyes settled on me, and I wondered if he was waiting for more.

"Would you like to write it down, Matilda?"

He looked across to where his white jacket hung from a peg. Up close and away from the distraction of Mr. Watts himself when he wore the jacket, I saw how grimy it was; it almost shone with its filth. The insides were slimy to touch. I found the exercise book and the pencil. Now I knelt down on the floor and entered my fragment.

My pencil-holding fingers had gotten clumsy. I was out of practice. My letters wobbled to start with.

I wondered if Mr. Watts thought I was taking too long over my fragment, because he called over to me. "When you finish, Matilda, return the book to my jacket if you wouldn't mind. And the pencil."

I looked to see where that tired voice had come from, or what caused it. I couldn't see Mrs. Watts' eyes. Mr. Watts' hand was covering them. I finished my fragment, returned the exercise book and pencil to their safe place, and left, quietly closing the door after me.

I DIDN'T TELL MY MUM THAT I HAD BEEN TO the Wattses' house. She would consider such a visit to be a betrayal. Even though I thought of myself as being in Mr. Watts' camp, it didn't mean I wanted to rub my mum's nose in that fact. I knew where the boundaries lay and I took care to step lightly around them.

And then sometimes I caught a glimpse of someone called Dolores, who was her own person, and not just someone's mother.

Early one morning when I crept up on her standing alone on the beach and looking out to sea, I knew from the stillness in her shoulders she was looking for something. Or possibly what she was looking for was floating on a tide of hope within her, and not out there in that huge baffling blue ocean-sky that separated us from the world.

Perhaps if we had been starving to death the outside world would have helped. We would have been an aid project. But we had food. We had our gardens and our fruit, and we had fish so long as Gilbert's father's boat was kept a secret.

Secrets were the last things we gave up. Our parents had stopped keeping from us the things they heard. They no longer cared. Discretion required effort, and what was the point? What did it matter when you had nothing, and nothing to look forward to? We were practically in the same state that the Bible says mankind came into the world as.

We washed our only clothes and sat naked waiting for them to dry in the sun. We got about barefoot. The roof of our shelter let in the stars, the sun, and the heavier downpours. At night we lay on a bed of sand carried up from the beach by the handful. We were never cold, though, or really that uncomfortable. The hardest part was getting through the boredom of the night.

My mum's pidgin Bible had gone up in flames, so at night, while I tried to summon passages from *Great Expectations* she did the same with her Bible. I would hear her mumbling in the dark, and I'd have to roll away from her and put a hand over my ear to concentrate on my own retrievals.

It was easier in class. For some reason, whenever one of us produced a fragment I could almost always remember another one either side of it. It happened this way for the others as well. As the list grew it was clear that Victoria, Gilbert, Mabel, and even Daniel thought about *Great Expectations* as much as I did.

When Mr. Watts read out my fragment on Pip walking up to Miss Havisham's, Gilbert suddenly remembered Mr. Pumblechook. He referred to him as a bullfrog, and it was Victoria who remembered the name Pumblechook; now it was Violet waving her hand madly. She had remembered something. Wasn't it Mr. Pumblechook who had taken Pip to the town hall to be apprenticed to Joe Gargery, the blacksmith? Mr. Watts broke into a smile. He was as pleased with our efforts as we were. We got noisy with excitement. Sometimes he would have to hold up a hand to slow us down while he recorded the fragments in the exercise book. After each entry he wrote our name.

*

I LAY IN THE DARK trying to put names to the things I heard in the night. The rasping call of the shining cuckoo. The lazy flip-flop of the sea—so much louder at night than during the day. The odd sharp voice, rising above the joyless croaking of frogs. A clip over the ear for some kid misbehaving, or maybe for simply being awake. The low neighing laugh of an old man. My mum's wakefulness.

"Hey, Matilda?" It wasn't much of a whisper. She meant to wake me. "Hey," she said, and this time I felt her breath on my face. She gave my arm a tug. "I've got something to tell you."

I was trying to decide how to answer. I was awake, as it happens, but it wasn't convenient to admit that just then. I was thinking about the visit of Mr. Jaggers to Pip's neighborhood in the marshes, trying to remember how Pip felt when told of his good luck. I was on the brink of retrieving this fragment when my mum continued, and what she said shattered all that had been building in my head.

"I suppose you heard. Grace Watts is dead."

*

IT MUST HAVE BEEN at an hour when even the birds hadn't woken that I heard the tramp of men's feet pass our hut. It was Gilbert's father and some other, older men. I saw their backs as they disappeared behind the schoolhouse.

They dug a hole up on the hillside for Mrs. Watts. They had no shovels. They used sticks and machetes to break up the ground. After that they used their hands and a broken oar to scoop out a grave.

When the time came to bury Mrs. Watts, every one of us—kids, old people, anyone who could walk—went up the hill to support Mr. Watts. I remember the soft footfall of feet, and the silence of the mourners. I remember the damp air that smelled of the forest, and the tinkling of the mountain streams dropping into shining pools. It was the world getting on with its business.

Us kids were free to stare at our teacher. We did not need to wonder what he was thinking and feeling because Mr. Watts did not shift his eyes from the hole in the ground. He had on his suit, and the same white shirt we always saw him in. Only he had washed it, and put it on before it was properly dry. So you could see the pink areas of his chest through the wet cotton. He had on a green tie we were seeing for the first time. He wore socks and shoes. His face was very pale. His beard fell clean off his chin as he hung his head over Mrs. Watts.

She was wrapped from top to bottom in some matting

that some of the other women had made. I happened to catch Gilbert walk around the head of Mrs. Watts to sneak a look. He looked away quickly when he realized I had seen him prying. My angry face wasn't really for Gilbert. It was for me.

I couldn't stop wondering if Mrs. Watts was already dead when I had rushed into their house that time. What if she was already dead as I knelt on the floor proudly entering my fragment into Mr. Watts' exercise book? It shamed me to think back to the disappointment I felt because Mr. Watts had not been forthcoming with praise. Poor Mr. Watts. As I looked up, Gilbert caught my eye and mouthed something at me.

I looked around at the assembled crowd. The men's faces sweated in the heat. The women looked down at Mrs. Watts with worry. When a small branch broke off from the treetops and dropped a long way down, nobody paid it any attention. If anything, that falling branch reminded us that something needed to be said. That's when I heard my mum offer a prayer for Grace. She recited the Lord's Prayer, though not all the way through. In one place she got lost. She closed her eyes and bit her lip and fumbled about in her memory until she found the missing lines. In the end she got there.

It must have been because the silence was unsatisfying that Mr. Masoi asked my mum to say the prayer again. This time she recited it all the way through, and with open eyes. Mr. Watts nodded and mouthed a silent thank-you.

Someone else remembered a line: "...from dust to

dust..." but then petered out. We were back to silence. We waited with our hanging heads, and it came back: "The earth was without form, and void: and darkness...everywhere..." Mrs. Siep lost the thread again. As Mr. Watts nodded his thanks she interrupted him.

"No. Wait!" she almost shouted, and we all frowned at a woman who would shout over the shroud of a dead woman. "No," she said more quietly, dropping her hand back to her side. "What I meant to say is this. What I want to say..."

She waited for Mr. Watts to lift his sad pale head.

"I knew Grace when she was small. This small." She placed her hand near her knee. Mrs. Siep looked around for my mum.

"That's right," she said. "We were all at the same school."

"And the nuns. The German nuns," said another.

"Mr. Watts," said Mabel's mum. "Your Grace was the cleverest of all us girls."

"Thank you," Mr. Watts mumbled.

Now one of the older men spoke up. "I knew her mother. She was also beautiful..." The man who said this did look up but feasted his eyes on an old memory of female beauty.

Others began to speak. They gave their bits of memory to Mr. Watts. They filled in a picture of his dead wife. In this way he learned of a girl he had never met. A girl who could hold her breath underwater for longer than anyone else. A girl who could speak German with the nuns. A tiny girl who once got lost. They searched everywhere for her.

And where did they find her? Curled up under the shell of a boat. A fleshy little crab frightened of the sun. Someone said that and we all began to laugh until we remembered where we were.

The big things came back to us, and the little things. Mr. Watts did not care how small. He learned what color ribbons his dead wife wore to school as a girl. He heard how she lost a front tooth. It happened as she lay prone on a canoe, daydreaming she was a fish, when the prow popped up and smacked her lip. He learned how proud she had been of her first pair of shoes. So proud, she carried them everywhere with her, preferring anyway to walk barefoot.

Mr. Watts leaned back. His jaw opened. I thought he was about to laugh. All us kids were hoping. In the end he settled for a smile. Still, he had looked up. We considered that the first step to a better future. And now he glanced at the treetops and didn't care if anyone saw his watery eyes.

For a while I had the impression that Mr. Watts would prefer to join his wife in the ground, but now I saw him happy to remain with us. Especially after hearing all those fragments to do with Grace. It was like adding kindling to a fire. We wanted to keep that thin smile on his pale face.

Mr. Masoi remembered Grace running up the beach bawling her eyes out. She was holding her finger up with a fishhook buried in the flesh. Daniel, who wasn't even alive then, clapped his hands and said he also remembered Mrs. Watts as a young girl. "She was climbing up a tree and I was climbing up behind her."

We all looked to see what Mr. Watts made of that.

"Thank you, Daniel," he said. "Thank you for that lovely memory." Just as he said to all the others.

The stories kept coming until he held up his hands to say, "Thank you, everyone. Thank you for your kind words. Such memories," he said. "My dear Grace. Now she will know she was beloved." He stopped there, but the words I expected to hear were "after all." Because for as long as I could remember, Grace Watts was not really included in the village. She lived with a white man, a man whom our parents didn't especially warm to. It was partly that, and partly the strange sight of her standing in that trolley towed along by Mr. Watts wearing a red clown's nose. We did not understand the reason for this, we had no idea what it meant, and so it had been convenient to think Mrs. Watts was mad.

My mum saved her own memory for last. She didn't share it with the others on the hill over the open grave. I was the only one who got to hear it, and it came later that night, hours after we had buried Mrs. Watts. She lay back, talking up at the crude roof that held out the night.

"Grace was the smartest of all us kids, Matilda. She always had her hand up. Blimmin' smart, eh. She seemed to know everything without first being told. There are some people in the world like that. They are born with a dictionary in them. Or an encyclopedia. Or six languages. I don't know how it happens, but it does. And when Grace won her scholarship to Australia we were so happy.

"We were proud because Grace was going to show the white world how smart a black kid could be. She went to secondary school in Brisbane. Then we heard she was at dental school in New Zealand. She was going to come back here and look after our teeth. How we looked forward to that day. But when she came back she was a different person."

My mum stopped, and it was clear that "different" didn't mean better. I thought maybe discretion prevented her saying more. But it was just the moment of someone recalling a painful memory.

"She told us she couldn't fix our teeth. She had stopped her training. Instead of a dental nurse we got Pop Eye. She used her scholarship to hook a white man. We did not know what to say to her; we did not know how to be around her. And I will tell you another thing, Matilda: we did not know how sick Grace was. We did not know anymore if she was black or white. There. That's all I have to say on the matter because now she is dead."

The thud was the sound of my mum's hand falling on the ground between us. In a matter of seconds I heard the heavy breath of her sleep.

I WASN'T SURE HOW LONG MR. WATTS' mourning would last. Some of us worried that he would not come out of his house again—that, like Miss Havisham, he would become stuck. So it was a surprise, three days later, when Mr. Watts sent Gilbert to find me and ask why I wasn't in school.

In class Mr. Watts waited for everyone to sit down at their desks. His smile was firm, as if to say he was no longer a grieving man. When we were all seated he held up a finger.

"Do you remember that scene when Pip is met at the gates of Miss Havisham's by a very discourteous Sarah Pocket . . . ?" He looked around at our faces to see if anyone did. "You remember, I'm sure. Miss Havisham informs Pip, cruelly, that Estella has gone to another country to be educated and turned into a lady. Admired by all, she tells poor Pip. And having cracked that egg over his head she then asks if he feels he has lost her."

We were always quiet when Mr. Watts spoke. We never

played up. But now we fell into another, deeper level of quiet. We were *quiet* quiet.

We were mice listening out for the scampering feet of cats. We had an idea he was speaking of Mrs. Watts. His anger was listed on behalf of Pip's suffering, but it came of his own loss. We waited for him to come out of that place of mourning. We saw him wake up before us. He blinked, and looked pleased to see us kids. "So. What else do we have?"

Our hands shot up. My own included. We all wanted to take Mr. Watts' thoughts away from his wife's death.

In the days that followed we worked hard to produce scraps of a vanished world. We walked around with a squint. "What's the matter with you blimmin' kids. Is the sun in your eye?" our mums would say. Of course I did not tell my mum about our project. She was liable to say, "That won't hook a fish or peel a banana." And she was right. But we weren't after fish or bananas. We were after something bigger. We were trying to get ourselves another life.

More than that, Mr. Watts had reminded us of our duty, and in language that made us sit up straight. Our duty was to save Mr. Dickens' finest work from extinction. Mr. Watts now joined the endeavor, and of course his efforts surpassed our own.

He stood before us and recited: *Pip is to be brought up as a gentleman—in a word, as a young fellow of great expectations.*

We were hearing Dickens. We felt a rush of joy. Mr.

Watts grinned into his beard. He'd just brought up to the surface a whole fragment intact. Word for word. Just as Mr. Dickens had written. It wasn't like some of our own poorly remembered and half-grasped efforts. He looked around at our impressed faces. "Does anyone remember who said that?"

Gilbert answered, "Mr. Jaggers."

"Mr. Jaggers, the . . . ?"

"Lawyer!"

Our chorused response made Mr. Watts smile.

"Correct," he said. "Mr. Jaggers, the lawyer."

I closed my eyes and stacked the words inside my skull. *Pip is to be brought up as a gentleman—in a word, as a young fellow of great expectations*. Miraculously, a whole sentence came to me. I waved my hand to get Mr. Watts' attention.

"Yes, Matilda?"

"My dream was out."

Mr. Watts moved away in the direction of the door. There was an agonizing wait while he deliberated. He started to nod and I was able to breathe again.

"Yes," he said. "Yes. I do believe you are right. Now, does anyone remember the next bit? Mr. Jaggers lays down the conditions. One, Pip must always bear his name of Pip. Two, the name of his benefactor must remain a secret."

Daniel raised his hand but Mr. Watts guessed his question.

"Ah, yes. *Benefactor* again. Well, it's a person who provides or gives to another."

"Like a tree?" asked Daniel.

Mr. Watts didn't think so.

"I know you were probably thinking palm oil, Daniel, but I think we will get ourselves lost if we go too far down that track. Let's just say a benefactor is someone who gives someone else money and opportunity..."

Our faces gave us away.

"Opportunity. Chance," said Mr. Watts. "The window opens and the bird flies out."

*

WE HAD DIFFERENT WAYS of measuring time. We could count back to the day when the redskins stood over us while we torched our homes. We could count back to the first bonfire. Others less fortunate could count back to their baby's death from malaria. Some would forever be stuck on that day.

If I tried hard and concentrated I could almost count back to when I last saw my father. He was standing on the edge of the airstrip, staring at the small white plane as if he and his battered brown suitcase had no business with one another.

My mum rarely mentioned my dad. Perhaps she thought it was easier this way, on her and me. I have no doubt that he occupied her thoughts, however, even more than her efforts to retrieve passages from the lost Bible. But the only time she spoke of my dad was when something went wrong, and then it was to mark him with shame. "If your father could see us now," she'd say.

After Mr. Watts produced the fragment on Pip's change

of fortune, I realized that a Mr. Jaggers–type character had entered my father's life. He'd heard about the copper mine needing men who could drive graders and tractors. The trucks winding up Panguna mountain carried fill between the mine and the tailrace. So that's what he did, only my father's truck carried machines and parts up from the depot in Arawa.

Six months after starting that job, he became the new storeman at the depot. My mum said it was because he was trusted. The whites didn't trust the redskins. The redskins took and gave to their own, and whenever challenged they produced faces that denied any knowledge of what they had done. Or so my mum said.

The new job meant my father had more contact with the white Australians. His English was good. I know because on a visit to Arawa I had seen him talk and laugh with the Australians. The white men wore mustaches, sunglasses, and shorts and socks. Their stomachs were large. And my father was trying hard to be like them, the way he stuck his tummy out. He, too, placed his hands on his hips to turn himself into a teapot. But it was when I saw him smile a sly smile, a white man's smile, that I knew. Well, maybe I am my mother's daughter for thinking this. I can't help what I saw. I saw my father sliding away from us.

The Mr. Jaggers in my father's life was his boss, a mining engineer, one of the many contracted. He was Australian but with a German-sounding name. I'd heard my mum and father discuss this man. My father called him "his friend." My mum said his friend made him drunk.

This was true. She said seeing him stand in that dock facing charges of disorderly behavior provided enough shame for a lifetime. She didn't need to go back for more. His drinking began with that storeman's job. This is one of the reasons why my mum refused to move from the village. She did not want to move to Arawa to see my father turn into a white man.

I remember she was in more of a mood to listen when he brought back news from Panguna. The situation up at the mine was serious and it seemed to get worse with the passing of every day. It spiraled out of control after the rebels got their hands on some explosives, which they used to blow up sections of the road. Some more time passed. We heard the rebels were armed. The Japanese had left behind a large cache of arms from World War II. We heard the rebels were restoring the guns. We heard there were secret workshops in the jungle where they worked on the rifles to make them like new again. Soon we heard that the trucks winding up Panguna were getting shot at.

By the time the redskin soldiers arrived on the island we'd heard enough rumors to make up our own minds about the future. The whites would leave the island while the government soldiers rounded up the rebels. But during that time the mine would close. There would be no work. No money. The man with the German name now presented my father, and us, with a way out. He offered to sponsor my father. *Sponsor* was the word he used. It was to be years before I properly understood that word. I remember asking Mr. Watts, who seemed to think *sponsor* was close to another word: *adopt*. This makes all the more sense when I think back to what the man was offering and what I had seen of my father as he tried to shape himself around the Australians.

I tried to picture the life he was leading in Townsville. Mr. Dickens' England was my guide. I wondered if there were beggars there. I wondered if there were smokestacks and thieves, and kind souls like Joe Gargery, who you might have thought were drunk for all the sense they made when they spoke.

I wondered if my father's stomach had grown. Whether he drank beer and wore shorts and a crooked dog's smile. I wondered how often he thought about us—his Matilda and my mum. I tried to picture the school I might have gone to in Townsville had we got out before the blockade. But I got no further than the classroom that occupied my life. I got no closer to Townsville than to whatever Mr. Watts and Mr. Dickens could tell me.

My mum now hoped to join my dad, whenever that might be. This was just wishful thinking, because there was no Mr. Jaggers in my mum's life. We were trapped, without a way off the island.

When I saw my mum down at the beach I knew what she was thinking—the sea offers the only way out of this life. There it is, day after lazy day, showing us the way.

*

THE WORLD MR. WATTS encouraged us to escape to was not Australia or Moresby. It wasn't even another part of the island. It was the nineteenth-century England of *Great Expectations*. We were working our way there on assisted passage, each of us with our own fragments, with Mr. Watts as helmsman sorting and assembling them into some coherent order.

I was extremely competitive about our task. It was essential that I come up with more fragments than the other kids. It would offer the proof to myself that I, Matilda, cared more about Pip than anyone else.

I can remember where I was and what I was doing for every fragment I retrieved. Otherwise, I have no sense of time passing in the normal way. Along with medicines and our freedom, the blockade stole time from us. At first, you hardly noticed it happening. But then you suddenly stopped to think: no one has celebrated a birthday for a while.

I was much better at saving my fragments now. I didn't need to rush to Mr. Watts' house with the scene where Pip leaves his village at dawn for his new life in the city of London. I could sit on the beach in the shade of a palm tree and see the moment clearly: Joe offers a hearty farewell. Biddy wipes her eyes with her apron. But Pip has already moved on. He is looking forward. *It was now too late and too far to go back, and I went on*... There, I had retrieved one of Mr. Dickens' lines.

In another hour it would be nightfall. If I was to use a stick to write the fragment in the sand I could stop worrying about it and run down in the morning to retrieve it. So that's what I did.

In the morning, before my mum was up, before anyone

could see it and steal it, or misunderstand it, I went down to the beach to get my words.

The world is gray at that hour; it moves more slowly. Even the seabirds are content to hold on to their reflections. If you look carefully you notice things that at a later hour you'd fail to see. This was always my mum's advice. Get down to the beach before the world has woken and you will find God. I didn't find God, but at the far end of the beach I saw two men glide ashore in a boat. They were full of quick movement for this hour. One of them, unmistakably, was Mr. Watts. The other, heavier figure was Gilbert's father. I watched them haul the boat up the dry creek bed. They didn't muck around. They didn't want to be caught by the dawn. They didn't want to be seen by anyone. And, as I didn't want Mr. Watts to see where I stored my fragments, I waited until they disappeared into the trees.

Then the only noise was the sand crunching under my feet. I found Mr. Dickens' sentence, shut my eyes, and committed it to memory before kicking away every trace.

*

ON MY WAY to the washing creek later that day I drifted into the area of Mrs. Watts' grave without thinking. I must have been in some sort of daydream. I don't recall. Or else my mind was a blank. A gray fog. I could hear the parrots and cockatiels and some thicket birds in the trees, but that's all until a voice called out, "Matilda. Are you on your way somewhere?"

"No, sir," I said. "I'm just walking."

"In that case, why don't you join me and Mrs. Watts."

As he rose to his feet I took in the improvements to Mrs. Watts' grave—the bits of white coral set around the edges, the scattered purple and red bougainvillea.

I wondered if I was supposed to say hello to Mrs. Watts. After all, the invitation was to join him *and* Mrs. Watts. I felt unsure what I should do or say, especially to Mrs. Watts, and sat down awkwardly. Mr. Watts smiled at nothing in particular. I watched a large butterfly flap onto a tree trunk and disappear. I snuck a look at Mr. Watts. He was still smiling down at Mrs. Watts. I needed to say something, so I asked him if Mrs. Watts had ever read *Great Expectations*.

"Sadly, no," he said. "She tried. But you know, Matilda, you cannot pretend to read a book. Your eyes will give you away. So will your breathing. A person entranced by a book simply forgets to breathe. The house can catch alight and a reader deep in a book will not look up until the wallpaper is in flames. For me, Matilda, *Great Expectations* is such a book. It gave me permission to change my life."

He leaned back as if to put our talk beyond Mrs. Watts' hearing.

"Grace, however, put the book down so many times she lost her place. If the phone rang it was like a prayer answered. Finally she refused point-blank to have anything to do with it. Well, not quite—she said she would read *Great Expectations* through to the end if I would try the Bible. So that was that."

I was encouraged by Mr. Watts' chattiness, and these

confidences he was sharing with me. There was another question I was burning to ask, and it occurred to me that this was the moment. If I could just summon up the courage. But I couldn't find a way of getting from Mr. Watts' disappointment in his dead wife's failure to love *Great Expectations* to why he used to tow Mrs. Watts behind on a cart. And why he wore that red clown's nose. The moment passed. A twig fell at his feet and by the time Mr. Watts bent to pick it up the opportunity was lost.

THE RAMBOS ARRIVED WITHOUT WARNING, their eyes bobbing in their black faces, mops of overgrown, ropy hair dangling with colored ties. These rebel fighters wore cutoff jeans. Some wore boots taken from redskin soldiers. I took an instant dislike to those ones. Most of them, though, went barefoot. Their T-shirts stuck to their skinny torsos. Some had button-down shirts with no buttons left or sleeves torn off at the shoulder. As with the redskins they carried their guns and rifles close—like next of kin.

Two popped up on the edge of the jungle. Three more came from the beach. One from around the corner of our shelter. Two more arrived from behind the classroom block. They crawled down out of the trees. No more than a dozen of them.

We were not sure how to receive them, even though they were our boys. The troubling thing is they'd snuck up on us, which wasn't seen as a friendly thing. But that wasn't all. They seemed to know about us. Had they been watching us? Had they stood in the shadows of the giant trees, listening to Mr. Watts talk of his wife's failure to read the book us kids were working so hard to bring back to life? Nothing they found came as a surprise. Neither our crude shelters nor the schoolhouse that lingered as some hard trace of the old and trusted world we had once known and walked about in.

They were our boys, but there were no faces in that lot that we knew. We watched them regroup near the jungle, some crouching with their rifles. You could see they weren't sure about us either. And their doubt made us afraid. So much was uncertain.

They seemed to know that the redskins had paid a visit. But they didn't know what had been said or given to them. We knew what had happened to other villages that collaborated with the redskins. In the minds of the rambos we might be such a village.

Gilbert's father padded over to them with some fruit. The rambos made no effort to meet him halfway. They stayed put with their rifles and suspicion. They were too far away for us to hear what was said. After a few minutes one of the crouching rambos stood up to help himself to a guava. The others watched him eat, and since he didn't drop dead they unfolded themselves from the ground, released their weapons, and followed suit. They were hungrier than they had let on. We watched them spit out the seeds and skin.

Mr. Masoi got their attention and pointed to the rest of us looking on like the spectators we had become. We had an idea Gilbert's father was offering them shelter and food. Though I imagine he as much as the rest of us was hoping they would leave, just light up out of here, because their presence made us a target for the redskin soldiers.

I have said we lost all sense of time. But I will guess. I will say the mine had been closed for nearly three years when those rambos came into our lives. That meant those boys had been living in the jungle killing redskins and fleeing from them for three years. We were the same color. We were from the same island. But living the way they did had changed them. They were different from us. We saw it in their eyes, and in the way their heads moved. They had turned into creatures of the forest.

Untrusting of open spaces they set up camp near the trees and away from the pigs. They kept to themselves until dark. I heard later they had asked for medicines, though I hadn't noticed any sick or wounded. I saw different people take them food. We were out to make a favorable impression.

The smaller kids willed one another closer and closer. One of the rambos would suddenly turn his head or hiss or clap his hands, and the little kids scattered like fish. The rambos rocked back and laughed, and that laughter was one of the more reassuring things we heard. Behind their betel-stained mouths and crazed stares, maybe they weren't so different after all.

That night they made a small fire. We could see their silhouettes rising and falling away into the dark, but they couldn't see us. Or hear our whispers. I lay beside my mum and I could feel the tension in her. I could hear the tightness of her breath. She would have liked to go over there and tell them to pipe down. Young ones were trying to sleep. The voices of the rambos carried in the dark. They were seventy meters away but sounded as if they were right next to us.

Some of them were drinking jungle juice; these ones grew louder and more boisterous. Real soldiers would have kept quiet and moved like shadows, which is how these boys had entered our village. But jungle juice has that effect. It made them forget who they were.

I watched my mum get up and arrange herself across the entrance of our shelter. I asked her what she was doing. She didn't answer at first. "They want girls," she said eventually. Strange. I had not felt included until she barricaded our sleeping place. Now I felt odd, like a piece of fruit that doesn't know it's fruit and therefore the object of someone's appetite.

It was the next day, just on dark, that they found Mr. Watts. My mum and some others, including me, were taking the rambos some food when we saw Mr. Watts heading towards us. Two rambos walked on either side of him. They couldn't believe what they had found. They used their rifle butts to nudge their prize forward. Mr. Watts looked irritated. He did not need that shove in the back. I watched him adjust his glasses.

One by one the other rambos leaped to their feet. Mr. Watts pretended not to notice the fuss. A drunk one rushed forward and in his mad jungle-juiced state shouted into Mr. Watts' face, "I will fuck you up the arse!"

I saw Mr. Watts stiffen and his head make a wary turn. He removed his glasses and studied them. As if his mind was elsewhere, on whatever he had been doing before being interrupted. The drunken rambo danced around Mr. Watts and made a crude finger gesture. Some of the others laughed, including the two who had found Mr. Watts. The drunken rambo had started to unbuckle his trousers. "I fuck you."

Mr. Watts had heard enough. In a very firm voice he said, "You will do nothing of the sort." Pointing back at the ground from where the rambo had sprung, he said, "You will sit down there and you will listen."

Mr. Watts did not look to see if he had persuaded the rambo. For him the man had ceased to exist. In all our eyes the drunk now looked like a ridiculous man. He knew it, too, because he turned away from our watchful eyes to do up his belt. The others moved to separate themselves from their companion. Then the rambo we felt might be in charge though we could never be sure—a solid man with one sleepy eye—got up from the campsite and approached Mr. Watts to ask him his name. He spoke pleasantly, and Mr. Watts answered without any hesitation. "My name is Pip."

"Mister Pip," said the rambo.

There were many of us who could have said Mr. Watts was lying. We could have stuck up our hands as if in class.

Instead we did nothing and said nothing. We were too shocked to dispute what he said. But as the man asked Mr. Watts his name, it was as if the word was already on the tip of his tongue—ready for that question. Of course, the rambos did not know its significance. They had never heard of Pip or Mr. Dickens or *Great Expectations*. They didn't know anything. For them it was simply another white man's name.

The rambo repeated the word *Pip* and it sounded like something unpleasant he wished to expel from his mouth.

Mr. Watts then began to recite from *Great Expectations*. "My Christian name is Philip, but my infant tongue could make of it nothing longer or more explicit, so I called myself Pip, and came to be called Pip."

I could not make up my mind whether this was spectacular daring or complete foolishness.

The man with the sleepy eye began asking questions. Where had he come from? What was he doing here? Was he a spy? Had the Australian government sent him? I heard these questions but I didn't hear any of Mr. Watts' answers. My mum had a firm hold of my wrist and was pulling me away. We were abandoning Mr. Watts. I was quite sure we would never see him again, and like my mum I was very afraid.

We ran the last bit to the beach. But where were we running to? The sea spread out to the far corner of the sky. We were stuck. There was nowhere for us to escape to but our shelters.

On dark we crept back like wayward kids now sorry for

thinking they could strike out on their own. Maybe that isn't quite right. It wasn't relief that we felt. Rather, we lay down in wait for some terrible thing we felt was about to happen.

After some time I heard Gilbert's father calling for me outside the entrance.

"Matilda, are you there? Come."

My mum answered for me. She said I wasn't here. That's when the large head of Gilbert's father poked inside. "Matilda," he said, "Mr. Watts wants you."

My mum told him I was staying put. Gilbert's father told her it was all right. He would look after me. He promised her. It wasn't what she was thinking. He said, "Dolores, I will take care of Matilda." I felt my mum release her grip of my skinny ankle.

Gilbert's father held my hand, but for all I knew his hand might be the same one that leads the trusting goat to its slaughter.

The rambos' campfire flickered and flared against the bumpy dark. I was noticing those sorts of things, along with my beating chest and my nervous sweat. As we drew closer it became clear that something had changed.

Mr. Watts was standing and chatting to the man with the sleepy eye. When Mr. Watts saw me he looked relieved. He excused himself and came over. His expression was somewhat perplexed, just as it was after Gilbert raised his hand to ask why Pip didn't *kidnap* Estella if he liked her so much. He placed a hand on my shoulder. In this way, Gilbert's father released me into Mr. Watts' care.

"Thank you, Matilda. I hope you don't mind. I want you here in case there is a need to translate."

Something had happened after we ran off to the beach and later slid inside our shelters like snails hiding from the world. In our absence Mr. Watts had asserted his natural authority. Already, I noticed, the voices around the fire fell quiet when he spoke. With his hand on my shoulder he turned me around to face those shining faces.

"You have asked me to explain what I am doing here," he said. "In a sense, you are asking for my story. I am happy to oblige but I have two conditions. One, I do not want to be interrupted. Two, my story will take several nights. Seven nights in total."

⁂

ON THAT FIRST NIGHT a crowd gathered, including the rambo who threatened to fuck Mr. Watts up the arse, all us kids, and our parents, who filed out of the shadows to stand at our backs.

Word had spread that Mr. Watts was ready to tell his story. Most of us had come to hear about a world we had never seen. We were greedy for that world. Any world other than this one, which we were sick of—sick of the fear it held. Others, gossips, came for different reasons. Everyone had a theory about Mr. Watts. My mum was there to hear about his life with Grace and, from her point of view, to learn at last how this unfortunate event had come about.

The first night was the scariest because we did not know

the depth of the rambos' interest or the length of their patience. They had invited Mr. Watts to explain himself, and this is what he set out to do, with his easy voice and delivery us kids knew so well. His one condition was that no one was to interrupt him.

Those rambos had not heard a storytelling voice for years. The boys sat there, with their mouths and ears open to catch every word, their weapons resting on the ground in front of their bare feet like useless relics.

Mr. Watts' decision to introduce himself as Pip to the rebels was risky, but it was easy to see why he'd made it. Pip would be a convenient role for Mr. Watts to drop into. If he wanted, he could tell Pip's story as Mr. Dickens had written it and claim it as his own, or he could take elements from it and make it into whatever he wished, and weave something new. Mr. Watts chose the second option.

For the next six nights I stood near Mr. Watts while he recounted his great expectations. It was a slow telling. Whenever his account departed from the one we knew, which is to say the one we were trying to retrieve, I heard a shift in Mr. Watts' voice. If I looked up I caught him glancing my way, which was his silent plea for me to just go along with whatever he said and not to dispute any of it. Sometimes he astonished us kids by using actual lines from the book—lines we recognized the moment we heard them. These were Mr. Dickens' lines not yet entered into the exercise book, and I'd have to restrain myself from congratulating him. He had known so much more than he let on when he set us the task of retrieving the book. For some reason I didn't feel annoyed, or let down. To have so trustingly closed our eyes in a bid to remember the bits of story that our wily teacher had known about all along.

Mr. Watts' story was to prove just as compelling as *Great Expectations* had to us kids. This time the whole village listened in wonder, sitting by a small fire on an island all but forgotten, where the most unspeakable things happened without once raising the ire of the outside world.

MR. WATTS' PIP GREW UP IN A BRICK DEPOT on a copper mine road without any memory of his parents. His father had disappeared without a trace, "lost at sea." His mum got drunk on jungle juice and fell off a tree inside the house. When she hit the ground her eyes bounced out of her skull. When she lost her eyeballs she also lost her memory. She could not remember what she could not see, and so she came to forget about Mr. Watts. Her next of kin were cane growers in Queensland, so that's where she spent the rest of her days, in darkness, walking among the clacking cane.

Happily, my translations improved with practice, and I began to relax when I saw people listened without noticing me. They held their heads at concentrated angles, their ears pricked like dogs that think they've just caught the sound of the broom headed in their direction.

The orphan, Mr. Watts, was brought up by Miss Ryan, an old recluse in a big house with dark rooms covered in cobwebs. Mr. Watts did not say much about his childhood. We didn't hear anything of school. We heard about a large garden. He would help the old woman with the weeding and planting. There was only one adventure.

For Mr. Watts' twelfth birthday, Miss Ryan arranged for a hot-air balloon to take the two of them high up above the house and its gardens. As they slowly rose in the air, he was amazed to discover a pattern in the garden. What he'd always thought of as a wilderness had instead been careful planting to resemble the pattern of Irish lace given to Miss Ryan for a wedding dress by the man who had promised to marry her. He then failed to turn up for the wedding ceremony. The man was an airline pilot. For all the years Mr. Watts was growing up under Miss Ryan's care, her beautiful landing strip failed to attract his plane.

Two days shy of his eighteenth birthday Mr. Watts came home to find Miss Ryan sprawled across the flower bed she had been weeding, her gardening gloves on her swollen fingers, her straw hat still tied beneath her chin, a ladybug crawling across her forehead, which Mr. Watts encouraged onto a leaf.

The old woman had no next of kin, and although she had never formally adopted Mr. Watts she left him her property.

Some time must have passed, and Mr. Watts must have accounted for it in some way. I no longer remember what he said or what I said on his behalf. Much of it won't be relevant anyway. So I will race forward to Mr. Watts' decision to turn the house into two flats. He rented the front half of the house to a beautiful black woman from this island.

Mr. Watts had never seen anyone so black. He had never

seen teeth so white or eyes that sparkled with such wicked fun. The young Mr. Watts was bewitched by her, by her blackness, by her white dental uniform, and she must have known this, he thought, because she taunted him mercilessly. She flashed her smile. She teased. She reached out and at the same time she danced away.

They shared the house. A single wall separated their lives, but if he placed his ear to it he could hear her move about. He became an expert at tracing her movements. When the radio was on he knew she was cooking. He knew when she was running a bath. He knew when the television was on and he pictured her coiled up on the floor with her feet tucked under her round bum, which is how he had once seen her when he came to collect the rent. Mr. Watts had a sense of her life but couldn't get near her for that wall standing between them.

While his nights were spent tracing her movements on the other side of that thin wall, Mr. Watts looked forward to Saturdays. On that day Grace washed her hair and clothes, and Mr. Watts came to know exactly what time to expect the whole sopping procession to pass by his window.

Winter arrived in the cold country. Great winds slammed into the side of the house. Trees were blown over. Rooftops were flicked off houses like bottle tops. In this weather Mr. Watts opened his door to Grace standing in the pouring rain.

My mum had her own theories. She said it was because Grace was lonely, and that it had as little to do with Mr. Watts as a free cup of tea.

Grace had come around to ask for Mr. Watts' advice. She was thinking of giving up dental school. She wasn't enjoying it, and for that she blamed the drill. All those open mouths and scared eyes. The eyes especially, she said. It was like unhooking a fish, only these were people.

That winter, the obstacle that was the wall was replaced by another—a wooden table that Mr. Watts sat on one side of, and Grace on the other. They were well used to each other's company by now. The table was in the way until one night Grace stood up and carried her chair around to his side. She sat down next to Mr. Watts, then she took his hand and laid it on her lap.

Some in the audience laughed. One person whistled. Mr. Watts nodded and smiled bashfully. We liked him for that. Some sort of romance must have followed, but Mr. Watts chose not to share that with us. Besides, we knew he and Grace had been a couple, so there wasn't any suspense to be gained by teasing that part of the story out. But he did have something new to share.

Looking around at our smiling faces, he must have adjudged there to be no finer or more appropriate moment than the present one. He touched his collar button. The white of his suit shone in the light from the fire.

"My darling Grace gave me great happiness," he said. "None greater than when she gave me a child, a baby girl to whom we gave the name Sarah."

Mr. Watts stopped here, but it wasn't the usual pause for me to pass on what he had said. It was so he could collect himself. He stared into the night high above the flames of the fire.

Everyone saw him swallow, and our silence deepened.

He nodded up at that baby girl. He smiled away, and we smiled with him. He almost laughed, and we were ready to laugh too, when he said, "We could not stop looking at her. We stood by the rail of her cot, looking down at her face." He nodded at the memory, then looked at his audience. "By the way, this is how white turns mulatto and black white. If you are the blaming kind, blame it on the horizon." Those who got the point laughed; some of the rambos followed suit out of fear they had missed something.

Mr. Watts continued.

"I have told you I came into this world an orphaned boy. I have no memory of my parents. I have no photographs. I have no idea what they looked like. But in that baby's face I thought I saw my dead parents emerge. I saw my mother's eyes, my father's cleft chin. I remember standing at the rail of the cot, staring with the hungry eyes of an explorer seeing new territory for the first time. It was familiar geography all muddled up. I saw bits and pieces of Anglo-Welsh heritage in a coffee-colored skin. Between us, me and Grace had created a new world."

I liked that idea. It encouraged me to think about my father. Perhaps he wasn't lost. Or we weren't lost.

If I'd owned a mirror I would have peered in it for a trace of my lost father. The still pools up in the hill streams did not offer the same detail. My face shimmered and darkened. So I sat on a rock and moved my fingers around my face. I thought I might find some telltale trace of my dad there.

My father had a rubbery mouth—from all that fat laughter of his, I guess. My lips were thinner, like my mum's, sharpened from making judgments. I traced my eyes but they just felt like my eyes. I found my ears. I have large ears and I will never lose them. They are listening ears. According to my mum, my dad had only ever used his to listen to his own booming laughter.

I decided that if I carried a trace of my dad it lay deeper than on the surface of things; maybe it circulated in the heart, or in the head wherever memory collects. And I thought I would sacrifice any physical likeness for the hope that he had not forgotten me, his daughter Matilda, wherever he was out there in the white world.

EACH NIGHT WE ASSEMBLED, SOME OF US sitting cross-legged on the ground, some lying with hands under heads to count the stars as they came out, one after another, like shy fish emerging from their holes in the reef. Some stood as if they might not stay (but they always did).

My mum was always the last to arrive. It was a point of pride with her. She liked to pretend she had her hands full with other, more important things.

That was the impression she hoped to give to anyone who might pay her the respect of noticing. She would wait until the last straggler had joined the audience. Only then did she allow herself the luxury of changing her mind, thinking she might have time to hear Mr. Watts speak after all, especially now that he had shown a capacity to surprise.

If you watched closely you saw Mr. Watts sink into himself. You saw his eyes close, as if reaching for faraway words, faint as distant stars. He never raised his voice. He didn't have to. The only other noises came from the fire, the sea murmuring, and the nightlife in the trees waking from their daytime slumber. But on hearing Mr. Watts' voice the creatures shut up as well. Even the trees listened. And the old women too, and with the respect they once reserved for prayer back when there was a roof to sit under and a white German pastor to stare at.

And the rambos were as enthralled as the rest of us. Three years in the jungle setting death traps for the red-skins had made them dangerous, but when I saw the soft focus of their eyes by the fire, I saw faces that missed the classroom. They were practically kids themselves. The one with the sleepy eye would not have been more than twenty. The rest were in their teens.

Nowadays I've come to think of them as no more than children in torn clothes bearing weapons from another war. But they had power. They had the power to ask the question that no one else thought to ask. The question was simple enough. *Who are you?* So in the first instance they were after information. In the second, they found themselves seduced by Mr. Watts' story. By the third night, it was settled. Mr. Watts was Pip and they—like the rest of us—were the audience.

Mr. Watts spoke with care so as not to leave anyone behind. Whenever he mentioned Grace's name we wriggled in to get closer to the story of one of our own in the white world. When Mr. Watts' voice started to falter we would know that the night's storytelling was coming to an end. His voice would stall in the middle of a sentence, at which point some of us would join him in staring up at the black night. This was a trick of his because when we looked down again we saw him disappear into the night, back to his house.

I won't try and mimic him here any more than what I've done so far. But the bones of his story remain with me, what I've come to think of as his Pacific version of *Great Expectations*. As with the original, Mr. Watts' version was also serialized, parceled out over a number of nights with a deadline in mind.

During this time Mr. Watts had called a school holiday, so us kids only saw him at night. This meant we were back to idle days to fill.

So when I saw Mr. Watts start up the hill one morning, I set after him. And it wasn't because I had a question to ask or a fragment from *Great Expectations* to share, or even to see if he was happy with my interpreting role so far. I followed Mr. Watts in the same unthinking loyal way that a dog gets up and follows its master or a tame parrot flies to the shoulder of its owner.

I caught up with him at Mrs. Watts' grave. At my approach he turned his head just enough to see who it was, and finding no reason for alarm went back to staring at the grave. I saw a mosquito land on his neck. Mr. Watts failed to notice or didn't care. I stood with him, looking down at Mrs. Watts' place in the earth. "Can you keep a secret, Matilda?" he asked. Without waiting for my answer he continued. "There is a boat coming on the night after the full moon," he said. "Another five nights and Gilbert's father will take us out to meet it. A few hours of open sea and we will be in the Solomons, and from there, well, I daresay, it will be up to you."

When I failed to respond Mr. Watts thought he knew the reason for my silence. "Your mum, too, Matilda," he then said. But it wasn't her that I was thinking of, it was my father. I would get to see him at last.

"Another thing, Matilda—this is very important. Don't tell Dolores until I give you the word." I kept my eyes on Mrs. Watts' grave though I could feel Mr. Watts' eyes on me. "You do understand, don't you, Matilda? Just nod if you do."

"Yes," I said.

He was inviting me to leave behind the only world I knew. While I might have dreamed of it, I didn't ever see myself leaving the island. I couldn't see the world wanting to take me.

He said, "You have nothing to be afraid of."

"No," I said.

"That's right. You don't. Please remember what I said, Matilda."

"I know," I said.

"Make no mistake, I intend to speak to Dolores. For now, though, it is our secret. Just you, me, and the trees. Oh, and Mrs. Watts."

⁂

ONCE MORE I found myself lying wide awake in the dark with a secret, while listening to the breathy sleep of my mum. Mr. Watts didn't trust her. And now, in effect, I had been told not to trust her either with what I knew; that in less than a week she would be leaving the island with me and Mr. Watts. And, who knew, it might be only a few more weeks before she saw my father again.

I ached to tell her. Once she asked me if there was something I wished to say because, she said, she could hear the wings of something flapping inside my head.

"Just thinking," I said.

"About?" she asked.

"Nothing," I said.

"In that case you might find time to go and ask Mr. Masoi for a fish."

I felt bad, knowing how much hope my news would give her. It would give her a reason to start thinking about my father in a different way. It would turn her thoughts to that outside world. It would force her to imagine her part in it. But I also understood—without any need for Mr. Watts to spell it out for me—my mum was a risk with that information. And I knew, even more than Mr. Watts did, what lengths she would go to score a point against him.

Around the other kids I felt my cheeks bursting with my secret, and at the same time I felt a sorrow. They didn't know that in less than a week I would never see them again. Part of me was already farewelling things—the trees, the floating sky, the slow tumbling hill-streams, the shrieking of the birds at dawn, the greedy noises of the pigs.

But Mr. Watts' secret plans began to trouble me. If

we were to leave the island my mum would need some warning—more than what Mr. Watts was planning to give her. She would be expected to make up her mind on the spot. I was afraid she would say no, and I was afraid of what I would choose.

I wasn't prepared to break my promise to Mr. Watts, but I felt my mum needed some mental preparation. The only way I knew how to help her was to tell her about Mr. Jaggers' visit to Pip in the marshes. This is the part of Mr. Dickens' story that has always stayed with me. The idea that your life could change without warning was very appealing. I suppose my mum would use different language. She would have said, as Pip later does, that her prayers had been answered. So this is what I talked about to my mum as we woke and lay like stunned fish beneath the splintered dawn.

I talked knowledgably, and quickly, about a world I had never been to, but felt I knew as intimately as this patch of tropical coast where we lived, and my mum listened, as anyone would, to have a bigger share of the world. What she heard about was Pip's readiness to leave behind everything that had gone into making him—his scarecrow sister, dear old Joe Gargery, pompous Mr. Pumblechook, the marshes and their murky light—everything that was home.

⁂

AROUND THE RAMBOS' campfire, the world Mr. Watts revealed to us was not from the island, or Australia or New

Zealand, or even from nineteenth-century England. No. Mr. Watts and Grace had created an entirely new space, which they called the spare room.

The spare room. This presented some translation difficulty. I talked about a womb to be filled, a hull to fill with fish. I spoke of the coconut hollowed out of its white flesh and milk. The spare room, Mr. Watts said, was meant for their coffee-colored child to one day call her own.

Before Sarah's birth they had used the spare room as a dumping ground for all the things they had no use for. Now they agreed to start again with it empty. They wanted it to be unspoken for. They wanted their vision of some unrealized place to inhabit the room. Why leave things to chance? they thought. And why pass up the opportunity of a blank wall? Why go in for wallpaper covered with kingfishers and flocks of birds in flight when they could put useful information up on the walls? They agreed to gather their worlds side by side, and leave it to their daughter to pick and choose what she wanted.

One night Grace wrote the names of her family over the wall, a history that went all the way back to a mythical flying fish.

For the first time since I'd started translating for Mr. Watts I was interrupted. Grace's half-blind grandmother asked Mr. Watts if her wayward granddaughter had remembered to write her name up on the wall.

Mr. Watts closed his eyes. His hand cupped his chin. He began to nod. "Yes, she did," he said, and the old woman breathed again. Now someone else—an aunt of Grace's—

stuck up a hand to ask the same thing. And so did another five or six relatives until all were satisfied their name was on the wall of a room of a house out there, somewhere, in the white world.

To Mr. Watts' suggestion they paint the walls of the spare room white, Grace scribbled *a history of white on the island where I was born.*

And now, to the startled ears of all us kids, we began to hear all the fragments that our mums and uncles and aunts had brought along to Mr. Watts' class. Our thoughts on the color white. Our thoughts on the color blue. Mr. Watts was assembling his story out of the experience of our lives, the same things we had heard shared with our class. But Mr. Watts introduced new information as well, such as Grace's thoughts on the color brown.

There were no brown ice-blocks until the cola one was invented, and then it came and went like a comet. When they were all gone Grace asked the man in the shop why and he said because no one wanted them. She said, "We do." He said, "You kids don't bloody count. Now bugger off."

Around the fire, the rambos slapped each other and hooted with laughter, and a lone dog, some way off, took up the call.

I began another tricky translation—Mr. Watts' thoughts on the color white. Miss Ryan once told him she used white chewing gum to steady a white tooth she had knocked on a water fountain before a date with the airline pilot who she remembered smelling of black shoe polish!

Mr. Watts paused, looking at me. He seemed very pleased with himself. It was obvious that he expected his audience would be charmed once I passed this on. But what the blimmin' heck was black shoe polish?

"Otherwise," Mr. Watts continued, "everyone in those days smelled of white soap."

I caught the eyes of Celia and Victoria. I saw I wasn't alone in what I felt. We were beginning to feel nervous for Mr. Watts. He wasn't making any sense. I found my thoughts escaping to *Great Expectations,* to Joe Gargery and the nonsense that had flowed out of him.

I remembered listening to Mr. Watts read and hearing words that on their own I understood, but once they were turned into sentences made no sense at all. When we asked for the meaning of Joe's observations Mr. Watts replied that we didn't need to know. If the blacksmith didn't make sense, *that* was the point. While that might be true, I was worried that Mr. Watts had now gotten his characters mixed up, that somehow he had slipped out of Pip and into Joe Gargery's skin. My translation failed to move the audience in the way Mr. Watts' self-satisfied smile hoped for. Instead, he found himself looking at an audience of dog-faces still waiting for the promised bone.

He recovered and spoke about a neighbor of Miss Ryan's who used to row flying-boat people ashore in the islands. The neighbor was holding a paintbrush dipped in white paint when he was found dead of a heart attack by the half-painted letterbox. Too much white sugar, we heard. Or was it salt?

So he was back onto the color white.

The whitest white, he said, is the inside of a toilet bowl. Whiteness is next to cleanliness. Cleanliness is next to godliness.

White, he said, used to be exclusively the color of airline pilots and air hostesses. As a child you first learned about the white countries.

Bread is white; so is foam, fat, and milk.

White is the color of elastic that keeps everything up and in its rightful place. White is the color of ambulances, voting papers, and the coats of parking attendants.

"Above all," he said, "white is a feeling."

I had fallen into Mr. Watts' rhythm and translated that statement without hesitation.

A fleeting thought can come and go with its license to surprise. Words written or spoken aloud have to be explained. When I passed on Mr. Watts' opinion about "white being a feeling," I swear the entire island fell quiet. We all had long suspected this but didn't know for sure. Now we were about to hear.

We waited and waited, and while we waited Mr. Watts stood rigid, his eyes sloping away from us. At first, filled with regret, I thought, for letting that door open. But then I saw him nod to himself, and in as frank and honest a voice as I ever heard him use, he said, "This is true. We feel white around black people."

It made everyone uncomfortable to hear this, and yet I suspect we wanted to hear more, but that's when Daniel piped up.

"We feel the same," he said. "We feel black around white people." And that snapped the tension. People laughed, and one of the rambos got up and made a drunk's walk over to high-five with Daniel. Daniel beamed. He knew he'd said something but wasn't sure what.

IT HAD STARTED WITH GRACE WRITING HER relatives' names on the walls of the spare room. Now the writing spread to other areas. Mr. Watts and Grace put up their separate histories and ideas. They argued like roosters. They wrote place-names. Kieta. Arawa. Gravesend, the arse end from which England shat its emigrants. That's how I would hear it described years later.

The young rambos didn't know that Grace's ideas were really ours—from here. I cannot remember them all. I do remember Mr. Watts complaining about her sentences sometimes forgetting to include full stops. A sentence would just break off and leave the eye to plunge into vacant space. When he raised this, Grace asked him, *What would you rather do? Sit with your feet dangling off the end of a wharf or have them shoved inside stiff leather shoes?*

I suspect only the more fanciful and weird lists covering the walls are the ones that have stayed with me. Some were mixed up together. The ordinary but possibly more subtle lists have drifted from memory. But these I remember.

Things that tell you where home is

Wherever memory sticks. That house window. That tree out front.
The red-necked stint, light as an aerogram, that flies the Pacific from top to bottom and back again, and always believes it will find home.
The easiness of strangers who ask, What do you know?
The noise of a bus changing gears two streets away where the road begins to climb all the way back to a moment in childhood.
The high winds that make everything windblown (paper and leaves) seem personal.
The ancient sea chart that looks like a string shopping bag containing lines to do with currents and prevailing winds.
The smell of rotten fruit.
The smell of fresh-mown grass and lawn mower oil.
The holy quiet of a man who has lived for seventy-five years on the one island and has nothing left to say.

The history of the world

Step one. You need a lot of water—from above and below. The water of heaven fills the lakes and rivers. Now add equal amounts of darkness and daylight. While there is light the sun draws the water back up to restock heaven.

Step two. Man is created out of dust. At the end of his life he returns to dust. Restocking again.

Step three. The most important ingredient of all. Take a rib bone and create a woman to keep the man company, righteous, and fed. Add a spoonful of sugar for pleasure and bitter herbs for tears. There will be plenty of both, and the rest just follows on from there.

A history of memory

I miss island laughter. White people don't laugh in the same way. They laugh in a private, sniggering way. I have tried to teach your father to laugh properly and he is learning. But he does not practice enough.

I miss the warm sea. Every day us kids used to jump off the wharf. But never on Sundays. You know why.

I miss the color blue, and fruit bats at dusk.

I miss hearing the thud of a coconut falling.

Broken dreams

The girl next to where I grew up used to sleepwalk. It was amazing how far she would get—still fast asleep. One time she paddled a canoe out to the reef, came in, and went back to her sleeping mat. Or else you'd see her marching up the beach like she was late for church.

Once we found her in our house sitting at the table,

her eyes closed, while every other part of her suggested she was waiting to be brought a cold drink. I was going to wake her, but my mum stopped me. What if she is dreaming . . . ? Dreams are private, she said. And she is right. A dream is a story that no one else will get to hear or read.

Thanks to dreams, in the history of the galaxy the world has been reinvented more often than there are stars.

The girl in our house, though, was probably just dreaming about jumping off the wharf—and that's okay too.

How to find your soul

If you tell your mother a lie you may do nothing more than blush, grow a bit hot under your skin. But later, at two in the morning, sitting in that dumb car you will begin to feel deceitful.

All that feeling has to go somewhere and it does. It has been stored in a vault deep in your body. Don't ask a doctor to find it. Like your father they are next to useless on these matters.

You need to know about hell. Don't ask your father. His geography is limited. Hell is less important to him than London or Paris. All you do is eat and shit and take photos in those places. Heaven and hell are the cities of the soul! That's where you grow!

Your shoelaces

Your shoelaces are useless on their own. They need a shoe before they can work. A human being without God is just flesh and blood. A house without God is an empty house waiting for the devil to move in. You need to understand boundaries.

Boundaries

Braids remind us that sometimes it is hard to know where goodness ends and badness begins.

Mr. Watts and Grace had agreed to gather their worlds side by side, to stick them up on the walls of that empty room and leave it to their child to pick and choose what she wanted.

But neither would admit that there were ideas and positions of their own they wanted their daughter to inherit, and that some were opposed to one another. I knew—probably everyone did—that Mr. Watts did not believe in God. We'd known all along without him saying so. We only had to look at him whenever my mum had come to lecture us kids on the devil.

In the class he stood behind her with his chin sliding down his chest, eyes closed, arms folded, as if barring himself against all of what us kids were hearing. Now, before the campfire audience, he openly revealed himself as a godless man. But he did so from the distance of the spare room.

If things turned nasty he could always claim to have become a changed man. A saved man.

There was spunk in Grace's voice—and humor that she managed to get up on the wall. Mr. Watts worried that Sarah would hear her mother's playful voice and that alone would make her want to believe in God. There was Grace's persuasiveness, but also, not to believe would be to betray her mother. Mr. Watts was in a bind. What to do? His own lists looked like study notes. They weren't fun. And they needed to promise fun if they were to compete with Grace's entertainments on the soul and the devil.

One night, at a very late hour, he crept into the room and applied bleach wherever the word *devil* appeared on the walls. Soon the word *devil* began to change to a light brown color. Mr. Watts was encouraged. The offending word looked like it might even fade away.

A few days after that he found Grace had run masking tape down the wall to separate the names of his favorite make-believe characters from those of her family. When we heard that, one or two of Grace's older relatives quietly applauded. The others made do with an approving nod.

We knew who we wanted to win the battle for the spare room, my mum especially. And when it came to laughs it was no contest at all. Here's a footnote that Grace added to her thoughts on broken dreams:

> A dog with the shakes is a sign. Sometimes a dog will get up and look around like it has been bitten

> on the bum by a flea. It is really looking for where its dream ran off to. Sometimes it will just lie down again and rest its snout on its paws and wait for it to return.

When they heard these little stories the rambos laughed and the whites of their shiny teeth showed up in the light from the fire. The donors of these fragments and anecdotes were left to smile to themselves in the shadows. One of them was my mum. In fact, much of what Mr. Watts said Grace wrote over the walls of the spare room was my mum's vision of the world, and much of it us kids had heard when she turned up to class to rattle our skulls.

On the fifth night Mr. Watts introduced to the wall a scrap we'd heard in class about Pip versus the devil. Again, only us kids knew the history of this debate. Now we heard what happened as it was thrashed out in the spare room.

Mr. Watts challenged Grace to describe the devil. As he announced this around the campfire I felt the breath of my mum on my neck, even though she stood some distance away. This was one of the times when I felt Mr. Watts was personally addressing her. He was about to thread their old classroom debate into his account of the battle for the spare room. And she was ready.

I was worried about what would happen if Mr. Watts used the occasion to get back at her. I was afraid that her unshakable faith would single her out from the rest of us. She would defend God and the devil even if it meant breaking the rules set by Mr. Watts. And I knew what would happen if she opened her mouth too quickly—all that would come out would be anger.

"So," began Mr. Watts, "how might we recognize this creature? Does he have horns? Does he produce a business card? Does he have a lipless mouth? And no eyebrows? Do his eyes have a wanton quality?"

By putting up these questions Mr. Watts was creating a devil before our eyes. And, as quickly as he had produced an image in our heads, he set about dismantling it with the same explanation we'd heard my mum give us kids. "We know the devil because we know ourselves. And how do we know God? We know God because we know ourselves."

My mum must have liked hearing that.

To those boys in the audience who knew what it was to butcher a redskin one day and carry a wounded brother over the mountains the next, it must have come as a relief to hear their blood wasn't all that bad. Those boys sitting around the fire were catching up to what us kids had already heard in class. The stalemate between Mr. Watts and my mum. The preparedness of Mr. Watts to believe in one made-up character (Pip) but not another (the devil). The conviction of my mum that the devil was more real than Pip. If pushed, she might have admitted that the illustrated versions of the devil—including her encounter with that witch from her childhood who turned herself into an ugly carnivorous bird—were just showbiz.

This wasn't Mr. Watts' story we were hearing at all. It wasn't his or Grace's story. It was a made-up story to which we'd all contributed. Mr. Watts was shining our experience of the world back at us. We had no mirrors. These things and anything else that might have said something about who we were and what we believed had been thrown onto the bonfire. I have come to think that Mr. Watts was giving back something of ourselves in the shape of a story.

*

ON THE SIXTH night, Mr. Watts told a tale, his own I believe, that established the place of the nonbeliever. I don't know if he gave it a title, but I will. I will call it "The Mayfly Story." If you were my mum you might have felt you were listening to an admission from a heathen that everything he had said or believed was wrong. I have come to think of it as his gift to her.

The Mayfly Story

> Some neighborhoods carry their history in their name. Wishbone Street is one of those. In this street lived a black woman, known to everyone as Mrs. Sutton, who measured her wealth in the number of dreams she had. Her know-it-all white husband, who was really only a woodwork teacher, which would have been okay but he was a bad woodwork teacher, said her wealth was worth nothing. With what can you buy a dream? How many dreams is an ice cream or a steak worth? He laughed and made fun of her.
>
> Dreams are nervy things—all it takes is for one

stern word to be spoken in their direction and they shrivel up and die. This is what happened. She had looked up at a critical moment in her telling to see her useless husband pick some sawdust out of his forearm hair. Now Mrs. Sutton tried writing the dream down on paper. As an extra precaution she wrapped the dream around a small stone she carried in her pocket.

Usually after cross words she would take herself off to a quiet place and wait for the shattered dream to return. Not this time. As she left the house her husband did not even look up. It was later, when she failed to return after dark, that he started to worry.

He waited for her to call because that is what he thought she would do. She would telephone from some lonely phone box somewhere in the night and ask him to come and drive her home. He waited and waited for that call. He waited until he could wait no longer and rushed out to look for her.

Someone spoke of seeing her walk in the direction of the river. Which now seems likely. Why? Because several days after her disappearance a slip of paper washed up on the banks and caught in the branches of an uprooted tree. Enough of the handwriting was legible. It seems Mrs. Sutton had dreamed she was a mayfly. Her husband, once a nonbeliever, was the only one to take the claim seriously. In fact, the once stupid husband was the only one to link the dream to his missing wife.

And he did more than that. At the library, where he'd gone to read up on his wife's transformation, Mr. Sutton learned that a mayfly will live up to three years in the mud at the bottom of a river.

For the next week he took himself off along the banks of the river, looking for a trace of his wife. He was a sad figure. We must imagine a man looking down at the water for the mud at the bottom. He supposed his wife would reappear when she thought the time was right. So he went back to the library to find out more on the life cycle of the mayfly.

He was not encouraged by what he read. On the day of its death the mayfly will rise from the river and turn itself into a winged insect. By then, the lazy bugger males have flown to the shade of the trees on the bank. As the females hover above the river they are rushed by the males. Once impregnated, the mayfly females fly upstream and bomb the surface of the river with eggs. As soon as that job is done they fall exhausted into the water. And there the frogs know what to look for.

It is hard to say which stage in the life cycle enraged Mr. Sutton the most. The waiting males or the greedy frogs.

A boy cycling home by the river saw Mr. Sutton wading up the river, his head bowed in concentra-

> tion. He was trying to see through the water to where he supposed his wife had buried herself with several million other larvae. Poor Mr. Sutton. He was shouting and carrying on as he attempted to hit the frogs with the many stones he carried in his pockets.

We loved that story. I don't know where Mr. Watts fished it up from. Maybe he made it up on the spot. We all laughed. The rambos hooted. They especially liked the bit about Mr. Sutton trying to hit the frogs. Everyone was laughing so hard they didn't see Mr. Watts seek out my mum with a smile.

ON THE SIXTH night we also learned that Sarah, the future occupant of the spare room, had succumbed to disease. Meningitis. As he told us this Mr. Watts' voice ran dry. For the first time as he stared into the fire the mask of Pip almost fell away. We were in no doubt here; we weren't hearing invention.

After Mr. Watts composed himself he told us how he and Mrs. Watts buried their child. For a long time the two of them stood clinging to one another over the small plot of piled dirt. Mr. Watts said they stayed like that until after night fell, and they had no more tears, and their tongues were idle because there were no words. No one, he said, has yet invented words for a moment like that.

"Grief," he said, and he shook his head back at the night.

He described Mrs. Watts' descent into depression. We heard how she could not get out of bed in the morning. She would not speak. Desperate for a remedy, Mr. Watts looked to the example of the hermit crab. How many times in its life does a hermit crab change its house? Three, four times? Mr. Watts thought that might be the answer. A new house, new windows with a different view. But what if her misery migrated with her? No. Mr. Watts decided the only way to mend his beloved Grace was for her to reinvent herself.

For the first time, we heard Mr. Watts ask a question of the audience. "I wonder, does anyone here know who the Queen of Sheba was?" He looked around our firelit faces. I was standing with my mum. I could hear her shallow breaths increase. I could feel her agitation rise, until every door in her was flapping open. She just had to speak up. And without raising her hand, which was how us kids had been instructed, she blurted, "It is in the Bible."

When he heard her voice Mr. Watts knew exactly how far to turn his head. I have an idea he always knew where my mum was in the audience. He smiled at his old adversary.

As he had in the classroom, he gestured for her to continue. By now other faces were looking our way. One of the rambos stood up and came forward, parting the audience with his machete so he could see who the voice belonged to. Now that she had the attention of everyone my mum suffered an uncharacteristic crisis of confidence. Her head dropped. Her voice wasn't as strong as before, and she addressed the ground rather than the faces looking her way.

"The Queen of Sheba was a very wise black woman who sought out Solomon to see if she could match his legendary wisdom with her own." That's what she said. She and Mr. Watts stared at one another, and it was Mr. Watts who chose to end it the way that he did.

He looked around the rest of his audience and began to recite from the King James Bible. "'She communed with him of all that was in her heart . . . and there was nothing hid.' "

SOME PEOPLE CAN LOOK TO THE TIDE AS A guide to the passing of the hour. Others look at a budding fruit and automatically know the month. On the edge of the silvery ocean, a pale thread of moon whispered to me: a new moon was on its way.

I had been patiently counting the days down to the two events—our departure, yes, but more important, that moment when Mr. Watts would choose to let my mum in on the plan to leave the island.

I was certain Mr. Watts hadn't spoken to my mum about it yet. She would have said something. There would have been some sign she knew, some lift in her mood. She would want to break the news to me.

I reminded myself what Mr. Watts had said about speaking to my mum. He wanted that job for himself. And that was fine. I just wished he would get on with it, because my mum deserved more time to prepare herself than what Mr. Watts clearly meant to give her.

I must have felt emboldened by what Mr. Watts had to say about the Queen of Sheba, the bit about her communing of all that was in her heart, because as the audience broke up I followed Mr. Watts into the shadows. I wanted to speak to him alone, so I trod lightly, careful not to disturb the earth or Mr. Watts. We were almost at the schoolhouse before he stopped and looked behind him.

I saw his great relief—it was only me, and not a ghost clutching a machete, standing in his footprints. "Matilda. Jesus," he said. "I wish you wouldn't creep up on me like that." As quickly, his relief soured. He looked impatient, as if he knew what was coming.

"Have you spoken to my mum, Mr. Watts?"

"No," he said, and he averted his eyes, pretending he heard something in the distance. Then he came back to me. "Not yet, Matilda."

Not yet. For me "Not yet" came a bit long after "No." That's when I understood or at least thought I did.

"I won't go without my mum," I told him.

He looked at me a long while, testing my resolve.

He was waiting for me to change my mind. He was waiting for me to take back what I had said. I stared at the ground like an ingrate.

"Of course not," he said at last.

But what did he mean by "Of course not"? He would tell my mum? Or he would accept my decision? I waited for him to explain himself.

"Of course not," he repeated, and carried on into the night.

I decided Mr. Watts was just tired from his storytelling, and it wasn't what I'd said as much as the tone I'd used to express myself. I was the baby chick that had spat back the worm. Perhaps he was letting me sit in my own pool of insolence, and in fact had every intention of speaking to my mum.

I could have run after him. I could have asked politely for some clarification. But I didn't. I knew what I preferred, and that was—I didn't want to know. Rather, I wanted to believe.

The next morning I woke to excited talk. My mum was on all fours talking to someone at our doorway, her large bum in my face. Outside I could hear other voices. My mum wriggled out to join them. I dressed quickly and followed after.

We walked to the edge of the jungle where the rambos slept each night. We stared at the trampled grass and the coals of the previous night's fire. They had left without a word or a good-bye. All that story had got up and run off into the night. We stared at the edge of the green jungle. A jittery thicket bird hopped from branch to branch, its small alert head turning left and right. We wondered what had spooked them.

My mum thought it was a good thing. Although we were used to them and they were accepting of us, we were pleased that they were gone. We thought we would sleep easier. Some of us had other concerns. Did this mean we would miss out on Mr. Watts' final installment? Would we find out what had become of the brave schoolgirl who returned all those years later in a trolley towed by a man with a red nose?

I decided to speak to Mr. Watts about that installment. I'd make sure he understood there was still an audience. The story didn't finish there. And I knew he had another night at his disposal before he and Mr. Masoi would drag the boat from the dry creek.

I waited for the sun to pick itself off the horizon. I was giving Mr. Watts time to wake up properly, when the red-skin soldiers filed out of the dark jungle. Their uniforms were torn, and many of them wore bandages. Their faces looked drained. I now know what kind of person those blank faces are attached to. Their mouths were irritable and sour. They hardly looked at us.

One soldier snatched a banana out of a small boy's hand. It was Christopher Nutua's little brother, and Mr. Nutua could do nothing but clasp his hands behind his back and turn his face inside out with shame. We watched the soldier bite into it and throw the rest away, uneaten. Their officer observed this through his ailing eyes and did not say a word.

We were still adjusting to the change of mood, when we saw they had a hostage. It was one of the rambos who had camped here. His face was a mess, beaten many times. But I was sure which one it was. It was the same juiced-up one who had declared he would fuck Mr. Watts in the arse. One of the soldiers pulled him out of line. The officer shoved him in the small of the back. He gave another shove and this time the rambo fell to the ground. That's when we saw his hands were tied behind his back. One of the other soldiers moved quickly to boot him in the ribs. The prisoner's mouth opened but we heard no sound. Just a gaping mouth that a fish stabbed with a knife will produce. Another soldier picked him up and gripped him by the throat so that the boy's eyes bulged with fear through the pulp and mess that was his face.

We were all there, an orderly, well-drilled crowd. As usual, we'd gathered without any order to do so. The officer did not appear as interested in us as he was last time. We were waiting for him to go through his roll and ask us to answer our names. But he was interested in one name only. He approached the rambo. He stood over him and, in a voice loud enough for the rest of us to hear, he said, "Point out here the one who is Pip!"

The rambo lifted his bloodied face. He raised a weary arm and pointed towards the schoolhouse. The officer gave an order, and two of his men grabbed the rambo by the arms and, half-dragging him, made off in the direction he'd indicated. To the rest of us the officer said, "I am finished with being lied to."

As we watched the soldiers and the rambo disappear I remember feeling preternaturally calm. This is what deep, deep fear does to you. It turns you into a state of unfeeling.

It was only a few minutes later that we heard gunshots. Soon the two redskins reappeared by the schoolhouse. They carried their guns on their shoulders and otherwise looked bored. Between them was the rambo. They must have untied his hands, because he was dragging the limp body of Mr. Watts towards the pigs. We averted our eyes for the next bit. But some of us were too slow to avoid seeing the flash of the machete as it was raised. They chopped Mr. Watts up and threw him in pieces to the pigs.

I am unexcited as I remember this; my body no longer shakes. I no longer feel physically ill. I have found I can reassemble Mr. Watts at will and whenever I like, and my account so far, I hope, is proof of that. At the time, though—well, that is a different story. I suppose I was in shock.

Everything had happened so quickly—from discovering the rambos gone, to the reappearance of the redskins, and now the killing of Mr. Watts. The events seemed to come as a package. There was no separating them; there had been no time to breathe between them.

The redskin officer looked around at our horrified faces. His glower was him telling each one of us that he wasn't bothered by what we had just witnessed. He pointed his chin in the air. Once more he said he would not be lied to. He would not tolerate it. The way he looked at us, we knew he was looking for fear. He was looking for someone to catch his eye. Maybe he would kill that unlucky soul for insolence.

We looked at the ground, as if we were the ones who should feel shame. I could hear him sucking his lips—he was that close, but that's not why he knew he didn't have to raise his voice. By now we were so fearful, he could have whispered and we would have heard him.

"Look up," he said.

He waited for each of us to pick our eyes off the ground. He waited for the last kid, and for the parent to give that little kid a nudge.

"Thank you," he said at last, almost politely. And in the same tone he asked us, "Who saw this?"

He stared hard at our faces, and I am ashamed to say I was one of those who dropped their eyes back to the ground. It was only when one of us spoke that, in spite of myself, I looked up.

"I saw it, sir."

It was Daniel, looking pleased with himself. He had beaten his classmates with the answer. The redskin officer stared at him long and hard. He did not know Daniel was slow. He spoke to one of his soldiers, who nodded to another, and the two of them took Daniel into the jungle. He went without complaint, swinging his arms at his sides. And for a moment it seemed none of us would complain. Then Daniel's grandmother spoke up, the same woman who had come to our class to talk about the color blue. "Sir, let me go with my grandson. Please, sir."

The redskin gave a nod, and the old woman—after replying with her own nod of gratitude—hobbled along on a bad hip behind another soldier, who looked annoyed to be asked to lead an old woman into the jungle.

Along our line a small boy began to cry. The officer snapped at the boy to shut up. The mother's hands hovered over her son. She wanted to calm him but she didn't want to move without the officer's permission. The sobs grew fainter on their own. And when the officer turned to our end of the line, the woman dropped her hands and pulled the boy into her legs.

The redskin officer appeared pleased by these events. As

though everything was going along very well, perhaps even better than he had expected. He shuffled in his boots and clasped his hands behind his back. He wasn't looking anywhere in particular when he spoke. "Now, once more I will ask you fools—who saw the white man die? Who saw?"

The silence was long and hot, and as I recall there was no bird sound.

There was no sound until I felt my mum move from my side.

"Sir. I saw your men chop up the white man. He was a good man. I am here as God's witness."

The redskin officer strode across to my mum and struck her face with his open hand. The force of the blow turned her head. But she did not cry out. She did not fall to the ground like a helpless woman. If anything she seemed to grow taller.

"I will be God's witness," she repeated.

The redskin pulled out a gun and fired several shots at my mum's feet. She did not move.

"Sir, I am God's witness," she said.

The commander barked out an order and two redskins grabbed my mum by her shoulders and dragged her towards our line of shelters. She did not scream. I did not hear her utter a word.

I wanted to go with her but I was afraid. I also wanted to speak out on Mr. Watts' behalf but I was too afraid. I did not know how to speak out or run after my mother without bringing harm to myself.

"You. Your name."

Up close I saw the filmy sweat on the officer's face, and his yellow eyes seeking out my fear the way a dog will smell it on another.

"Matilda, sir."

"Are you related to this woman?"

"She is my mother, sir."

When he heard that, the officer yelled out to his men. A soldier came forward and pushed me with the butt of his rifle. "Move," he said. He kept pushing me with the butt. But I knew where I was to go.

When I came around the huts my mum was on the ground. A redskin was on top of her. Another soldier was doing up his trousers—this one looked cross to see me. He shouted something at the soldier who had pushed me here. This man said something in reply, and the one doing up his trousers smiled. The man on top of my mum looked over his shoulder, and the soldier who had brought me said, "Her daughter." Now my mum came to life.

She pushed the man off her. I saw her naked and felt so ashamed for us both that I began to cry. My mum pleaded with the soldiers.

"Please. Have mercy. See. She is just a girl. She is my only girl. Please. I beg you. Not my darling Matilda."

One of the soldiers swore at her and told her to shut up. The one I'd seen on top of her now kicked her hard in the ribs and she collapsed, gasping, on the ground. The soldier who brought me there grabbed my arm and held me.

My mum struggled to sit up, wheezing and groaning with the effort. She held out her hand to me. I saw how everything in her face had come loose with fear. Her wet eyes, the shapeless mouth. "Come here," she said. "Come here, my darling Matilda. Let me hold you."

The soldier let me go a bit, then snatched me back like a fish on the end of a line. The others laughed.

I felt relieved when the officer with the sweating face appeared. He seemed to find the sight of my mum crumpled up in the dust disagreeable. His eyes and mouth joined in disgust. He ordered her to stand. My mum struggled upright. She clutched her ribs. I wanted to help her, but I could not move. I was rooted to the spot.

The officer seemed to know exactly what I was feeling and thinking. He gave me a funny look—not quite a smile, but a look that has stayed with me ever since. He took a rifle from one of his men and with the barrel lifted my dress. My mum sprang at him. "No. No! Please, sir. I beg you."

A soldier grabbed her by the hair and pulled her back.

God's witness had changed back to a mother, but the officer didn't see that. He only saw the woman who had promised to be God's witness. He spoke quietly, as a man might who is in control of himself.

"You beg me, and for what? What will you give me to save your daughter?"

My mum looked broken. She did not have anything to give. The officer knew this, and that's why he was smiling. We had no money. We had no pigs. Those pigs belonged to someone else.

"I will give myself," she said.

"My men have had you. You have nothing left to give."

"My life," replied my mum. "I will give you my life."

The officer turned to look at me.

"Did you hear that? Your mother has offered her life for you. What do you say?"

"Don't speak, Matilda. Do not say anything."

"No. I want to hear," said the redskin. He had placed his hands behind his back. He was enjoying himself. "What do you say to your mother?"

While he waited for me to say something my mum used her eyes to plead with me, and I understood. I was to say nothing. I was to pretend that my voice was my secret.

"I am running out of patience," said the officer. "Is there nothing you want to say to your mother?"

I shook my head.

"Very well," he said, and gave a nod to his soldiers. Two of them lifted my mum and hauled her away. I went to follow, but the officer put out a hand to stop me.

"No. You stay here with me," he said. Once more I saw how yellow and bloodshot his eyes were. How sick he was with malaria. How sick of everything he was. How sick of being a human being.

"Turn around," he said. I did as he ordered.

All the lovely things in the world came into view—the gleaming sea, the sky, the trembling green palms.

I heard him sigh. I heard him rustle around in his shirt pocket for a cigarette. I heard him strike a match. I smelled the smoke, and I heard him make that kissing sound as he smoked. We stood there, almost shoulder to shoulder, for what felt like a long time but was surely no more than ten minutes. Over that time he didn't speak. He had no words for me.

So much of the world seemed to lie elsewhere. So much of it unrelated to our being there and what was happening behind our turned backs. Those tiny black ants crawling over my big toe. They looked like they knew what they were doing and where they were going. They didn't know they were just ants.

Again I heard the redskin officer sigh. I heard him sniff. I heard a murmur of satisfaction from him; it came from a deep place like a tummy rumble, and I thought he was giving his assent to an event that only he could see.

I found out later what I didn't see. They took my mum to the edge of the jungle, to the same place they'd dragged Mr. Watts, and there they chopped her up and threw her to the pigs. This happened while I stood with the redskin officer, listening to the sea break on the reef. This happened while I gazed up at a sky where I hardly noticed storm clouds gathering for the brightness of the sun in a blue sky. The day held so many layers, almost too many things, contradictory things, all jumbled up, that the world lost any sense of order.

In recalling these events I do not feel anything. Forgive me if I lost the ability to feel anything that day. It was the last thing to be taken from me after my pencil and calendar and shoes, the copy of *Great Expectations,* my sleeping mat and house, after Mr. Watts and my mother.

I do not know what you are supposed to do with

memories like these. It feels wrong to want to forget. Perhaps this is why we write these things down, so we can move on.

Even so, this hasn't stopped me from wondering if things might have turned out differently. There was an opportunity. My mother could have held her tongue. The question I keep coming back to is this: would my rape have been such a high price to pay to save the life of my mum? I do not think so. I would have survived it. Perhaps the two of us.

But at this point I am always reminded of what Mr. Watts once told us kids about what it is to be a gentleman. It is an old-fashioned view. Others, and these days I include myself, will want to substitute *gentleman* with *moral person*. He said that to be human is to be moral, and you cannot have a day off when it suits. My brave mum had known this when she stepped forward to proclaim herself God's witness to the cold-blooded butchery of her old enemy, Mr. Watts.

WE WERE ALIVE, I SUPPOSE. THAT WAS US moving like ghouls to complete the burial tasks, our mouths and hearts stunned into silence. I suppose I must have breathed. I do not know how. I suppose my heart must have continued to pump blood. I did not ask it to. If I'd known about a switch to pull in order to turn off the living part, I might have reached for it.

People waited until they were sure the redskins had gone far into the jungle. Once they were sure, they killed all the pigs. It was the only thing we could think to do to give a decent burial to Mr. Watts and my mum. We buried the pigs.

They found Daniel later that afternoon, on a mountain track, high in a tree, his limbs spread like a crucifix, ankles and wrists tied to branches above and below; a stick of wood holding his mouth open, and flies buzzing around his flayed body. They buried him with his grandmother.

I was aware of people both watching me and watching after me. I was aware of a dozen small kindnesses.

When night came I lay down but there was no sleep.

There were no tears either. I lay on my side, and I stared at the space where my mum should be, at the moonlight shining on her teeth, at her silent triumph.

I must have slept, though, because I woke to a wind from a strange direction. It rose, it turned shrill, it went mad with a thousand furies before neatly falling away to nothing. This was followed by a heavy rolling thunder of such violence that you thought it would bring the skies tumbling down. I don't imagine anyone slept through it. There was a rip of lightning. Then, like before, a tremendous stillness fell over everything: us, the birds, the trees.

A shiver passed across the sea, and it began to rain. This was no ordinary rain. This was not the kind that blows in off the sea and forces you to shelter behind a tree. This rain dropped down like flung stones. In the pale morning light I watched it kick up mud on the trampled ground outside. It was as if the gods were seeking to erase the wickedness that had taken place.

Rain in the tropics is warm, and like other rains I was sure it would soon pass. I had some things I needed to do that wouldn't wait. I needed to go up the hill and break the news of Mr. Watts' death to Mrs. Watts. Mr. Watts would want her to know. Under the trees the weather wouldn't be so bad. There was just this open ground to get across, and all that dancing mud.

I didn't run as I might have on other occasions when it rained. I didn't run because I didn't care about getting wet. Let the rain come down. I did not care. I might not care about anything ever again. Then I saw where I was headed and changed direction at once to avoid the place where we'd buried the pigs.

Of course, the damage was done. Thinking about the pigs unblocked other thoughts, and once more I saw the limp body of Mr. Watts. I saw the flash of the machete. I saw the body of the rambo roll over the edge of the pig's pit, casually kicked aside, of no further use to the redskins now that he had revealed the mystery man, Mr. Pip. I saw the redskin on top of my mum, his shiny arse, the roll of trousers around his ankles. I heard my mum grunt, a noise I still cannot get out of my head. I smelled tobacco; and in the mud splattering around me I thought I heard again the lip-sucking noise the officer made while he stood with me looking back at the beautiful world.

This is how I came to be walking without much thought to direction, without much care or idea of where I was headed—except I walked fast. I was trying to walk away from these thoughts. That's what I was doing. If I'd had my wits about me I'd have realized I was walking towards the gorge.

That's what I could hear through the trees, the heavy flow of a swollen river. I did not connect the two events: the rain and the river. The rain barely registered with me other than *I am getting wet*. But on thinking about it, this rain was wetter and more persistent than any I have ever known. It was rain that insists you take it more seriously; pay closer attention to it.

When I came to the river, I took no notice of the signs, the swift changes. One moment the river was fifty meters to my left. The next it was there at my elbow, a foaming brown tide of debris and trees with stricken branches surging for the open sea.

A river in flood is not the smooth, aluminum-coated phenomenon seen on television. It bulges, it spins. It is furious with itself. It gets caught up in whirlpools, then extracts itself; it releases itself from tight bends; it rushes banks, greedily clipping soil into its speeding waters. It catches everything in its path. It could even catch me.

It could catch me and I wouldn't care. I wouldn't care because everything dear to me had been taken away—my mum and Mr. Watts. My father was somewhere out there in a world I had no hope of reaching. I was alone. The river could catch me and I wouldn't care.

I was flirting with this notion of being caught and taken when, in the same moment, a wall of water about knee-high raced towards me. I could have moved to higher ground if I'd hurried. But I didn't. And it wasn't because I had decided to die. It was because I had never seen anything like it.

Something solid thumped my knee, probably a heavy piece of wood. I didn't see it. In spite of everything I have said about my numbness, the pain was sharp. Instinctively I raised my knee, clutching it, and in the next moment the flood picked me up as it had other bits of flotsam and fed me into the river.

There is a story that my father taught me to swim by throwing me off the wharf. That's why my mum says I was born with water wings. Without them I would have sunk like a stone. So I was not afraid of water. What I felt was a pure astonishment. The speed of it. Only a few seconds earlier I had been standing on land. Now I felt myself scooped up and dropped into a stronger current. I was part of this rush to the sea. I began to feel curious.

It occurred to me I could simply end things this way. I could just give up, let go. This is what the flood wished me to do, and I was thinking how, so far, it was all so easy, when without warning the river changed character. Suddenly I was being dragged under.

At last I knew what to do. I had to survive.

This is something we all take for granted, but no matter how bad things get, the moment you are denied air you fight for it. You know at last what you need. You need air.

I couldn't see anything for the silt in my eyes. The river was animal-like. It had limbs with claws. It had a hold of my legs. It pulled me down. I had to fight my way to the surface and fill my lungs with air. Then the same thing happened all over again. It grabbed my legs and pulled me down. It wouldn't leave me alone. I was pushed under countless times and was thinking what a dumb way to go. How careless of me. How stupid.

I saw my father's head wilt as he was given the news of my drowning. And as the last of the air drained from me it was the thought of my father's pain that drove me back to the surface. An hour earlier I couldn't have cared what happened to me. That had passed. Now I felt a responsibility to live.

At some point I bumped against something large and

solid. In the blinding confusion I thought, Yes, thank you, God, I've been thrown against a bank. Land. I could feel its certainty, its beautiful certainty. I threw my hand out and found myself clinging to a monstrous log.

I do not know what kind of tree it had once been. It had no leaves or branches. The water had turned its bark smooth. So it was spongy to touch. It was just a log, but in this situation, in this rushing water, just-a-log was a great deal more than just-a-girl. For one thing, the log would survive. No matter how many times it was turned in a current or shot forward on a rapid, it would eventually wash up on a beach. And that would be its story as it dried out in the sun, sinking further into the sand with the passing of each day. It would survive. I thought it might be worth clinging on to.

For a time we shot along to where the river split in two. Log and me drifted into the left lane (I will call it), which was a stroke of luck because this stretch of water shifted us out of the strong, nagging mid-river current into the still brown water spreading from the coast.

What would you call a savior? The only one I knew went by the name of Mr. Jaggers. And so it was natural for me to name my savior, this log, after the man who had saved Pip's life. Better to cling to the worldliness of Mr. Jaggers than the slimy skin of a water-soaked log. I couldn't talk to a log. But I could talk to Mr. Jaggers.

The river emptied into a vast area of still, flat water. I thought we must have drifted near the old airfield long since overgrown. That was okay. I was no longer afraid. We were going to survive. The thought came and went, but without any of the gratitude I would have shown earlier when the river was doing its best to hold me under. No. We were going to survive, and now it only felt inevitable, and business as usual.

I was one of those heart seeds us kids had heard about in class. I was at some earlier stage of a journey that would deliver me to another place, to another life, into another way of being. I just didn't know where or when.

In the near distance I could make out the schoolhouse. If only I could steer Mr. Jaggers in that direction, I might slip off and climb onto the roof.

The rain stopped. The gluey air was breaking up to high cloud. Above me I could hear the thudding of rotor blades. I closed my eyes and waited for the redskins to shoot. I was sure they would. They would see me and that would be that. A second later the helicopter thudded damply away behind the clouds.

It began to rain again. Slow, steady rain, and the schoolhouse disappeared behind a gray mist. I clung to Mr. Jaggers, now no longer sure where we were or of the direction we were moving in.

I started to worry that we would be brought back to the river and that the current would snatch us back into its path. Then we would be carried out to sea, where I'd be too tired to fight. That's what I was thinking when out of the gray mist arrived the sound of paddles and then the dark shape of a prow. One man was paddling—I knew him! Now I saw Gilbert and his mum, and someone else, an older woman. I waved my hand and called out.

Within minutes I was hauled aboard the boat, to the wonderful lightness of the world above water. I was hugged. My face patted and kissed. For the first time I was aware of the bone-ache in my arms.

I leaned over the side to look for my savior. Mr. Jaggers seemed to know with sad recognition that it was just a log and that the disloyal Matilda who had clung to its back throughout this watery trial was the privileged one, the lucky one.

For a few minutes after I was hauled aboard, the log drifted alongside—bobbing and sticking close. Every now and then one end of it lifted on a wave, and it seemed almost to inquire if there was room enough for it too. But no one else aboard looked at the log.

After each of them gave me a hug (even Gilbert), Mrs. Masoi smiled at me through teary eyes. She pressed her cheek against mine. Mr. Masoi didn't say anything. He had other things on his mind. He whispered to us to stay quiet. Then he turned the boat around and we headed out to open sea.

I found out later they had been waiting for darkness. And Gilbert's father had actually given word that they would start out for sea, when I was spotted clinging to Mr. Jaggers.

*

IN THE NIGHT I woke to men's voices. Low, unhurried, gentle voices. A large shape with a blinding light loomed up alongside us in the darkness. That light was magical but much too bright. A pair of powerful hands reached under my arms. They may have belonged to Gilbert's father or another man. I don't know. But I do know this. The first pair of eyes to stare back at me came from a black face. I could tell from their expression that something was wrong. I have often wondered what that person saw, or thought he saw. I only remember that he wore shoes. Shoes.

I felt myself relax. I was safe. I'm sure I must have felt glad. After all, we had been saved, fished out of the sea. But I'm guessing, because whatever I felt at the time has since contracted to a few enduring details. The boat that belonged to Gilbert's father, the same one I had seen Mr. Watts and Gilbert's father haul up the beach, seemed so very small when I looked down on it from the deck of the bigger boat. I remember being given a cup of something sweet. It was hot chocolate. After the sight of those shoes, hot chocolate was my second experience of the outside world. And this was quickly followed by a soft mattress under me, and the low purr of an engine.

We put in at a place called Gizo. A dawn sun was already burning away the fog from the hills. We could see a roofline of houses in among the trees. I heard a dog bark. As we roped up at a pier a dozen little black kids came running and laughing towards us. Behind them marched several figures in uniform. Men in smart shirts. We spent the night in this town. We must have spoken among ourselves.

We must have congratulated each other for our escape. I like to think we singled out Mr. Masoi for special praise. If we did these things I no longer remember them.

The next morning we set out for Honiara, the Solomons' capital. We were greeted by several policemen and taken to the infirmary. There, a white doctor inspected me. He asked me to open my mouth wide and he shone a light down my throat. Then he looked my skin over. He looked in my ears. He parted my hair. I don't know what he was looking for. He found a different light to shine into my eyes. I remember him saying, "Matilda, that's a nice name," and when I smiled he asked me what I was smiling at.

I shook my head. I would have to tell him about Mr. Watts and I wasn't ready to yet. I didn't want to mention Mr. Watts just because another white man had commented on my name.

The doctor took my temperature. He listened to my lungs and my heart. He was sure there was something the matter. He just couldn't find out what. His room was filled with so many things. Paper. Pens. Files. Cabinets. There was a large color photograph of him playing golf. He stood crouched over his putter with the same pinched look of concentration he used to comb over my body.

I noticed a calendar on the wall. I asked if I might look at it. I discovered it was September. To illustrate the month there was a photograph of a white couple walking hand in hand along a sandy beach. The year was 1993. I worked out that I'd missed my fifteenth birthday.

The doctor sat back in his chair. He pushed away from

his desk so that his white knees rose above it. He arched his hands under his chin. It was a kind face that studied me.

"Where is your father, Matilda?"

"Australia."

"Australia is a large country. Where in Australia?"

"Townsville."

Now he unfolded his legs and leaned forward to pick up a pen.

"And your father's full name is?"

I told him, and watched him write it out. Joseph Francis Laimo.

"My mother is Dolores Mary Laimo," I said.

Then he sat back as he had before and studied me over his arched hands and white knees.

"Why don't you tell me about your mum, Matilda."

I REMEMBERED MY FATHER'S DESCRIPTION as he looked out the airplane window and saw how tiny our home was. Now I knew what he meant when he said the plane rolled over on its side without falling out of the sky, and how the window filled up with view.

I saw the green of Honiara and its rooftops, and as we went higher it grew smaller and smaller until all I could see was blue. I was leaving for Townsville, to be with my father.

I knew all about departure. I knew from Pip about how to leave a place. I knew you don't look back.

I didn't get to see Gilbert and his family again. I don't know what happened to them. Only good things, I hope.

We were so many hours up in the air. The cool cabin was another new experience, to feel goose bumps. I am sure I dozed off, because when I next looked out the window there was Australia, flat, pegged out, and gray like a skin. It wasn't so far away after all. I kept waiting for the plane to land, but it took many hours before it dropped in the air. The knot in my stomach had nothing to do with the descent, though. I was hoping that my father would like me. I was hoping that I would live up to his memory of me.

I had on new shoes, a new skirt, and a new white blouse. In a paper bag I carried my old skirt and old blouse, practically rags, and a toothbrush.

A black man is easily spotted in Townsville, especially at the airport, and there he stood in the door of the terminal, waving both arms, his face one big shining smile. From the tarmac there was time to note some changes in him, and I felt my mum's critical side in me.

His transformation into a white man was near complete. He wore shorts, and boots that rose no higher than his ankles. A white shirt did little to hide his bulging stomach. My father and beer liked each other. That's what my mum used to say.

A man with flags had directed the plane to its park on the tarmac. Now it was my father's turn to stand as the flagman had, his arms held open to me. I didn't know what to do with my face. I wanted to smile, but instead my eyes grew hot, and before I knew it there were tears. These were happy tears.

My father wore a silver chain around his neck. After a hug he took it off and slipped the chain over my head. I think he just felt the need to give me something, and that chain was handy. I still wear it today.

"Look at you," he said. "Look at you." He turned around to the airport crowd with his beaming face and white teeth, as if to invite others to admire me. He asked if I had any luggage.

"Just me and this," I said, holding up the paper bag. He picked me up under the arms and spun me around. I didn't know if he had been told about my mum. For all I knew he had been expecting her to get off that plane with me. He didn't say, and gave little away.

My father placed a hand on my shoulder to direct me inside the terminal out of the hot Townsville sun. That's when I saw him turn his head and glance across the empty gray tarmac to the plane. And when he saw me notice that, he smiled through his glassy eyes and changed the subject. "We've got some eating to catch up on," he said. "I've bought you a birthday cake for each of your birthdays I missed."

"That's four cakes," I said.

He chuckled, and we walked into the terminal and its cool air, my father's hand on my shoulder.

*

I WENT TO the local high school. I had several years to make up, and at first I sat in a class among white kids younger than me.

On my second day I went along to the school library to see if it had *Great Expectations*. I found a copy sitting on a shelf—not hidden or in a "safe place," but there for anyone to come along and pick it up. It was a hardback. It looked indestructible. I carried it to one of the tables and sat down to read.

It was more wordy than I remembered. Much more wordy, and more difficult. But for the names I recognized on the pages I might have been reading a different book. Then an unpleasant truth dawned on me. Mr. Watts had read a different version to us kids. A simpler version. He'd stuck to the bare bones of *Great Expectations,* and he'd straightened out sentences, ad-libbed in fact, to help us arrive at a more definite place in our heads. Mr. Watts had rewritten Mr. Dickens' masterwork.

I puzzled my way through this new version of *Great Expectations,* underlining each word of every sentence with the stub of my finger. I read very slowly. And when I got to the end I read it once again to make sure I understood what Mr. Watts had done, and that any disappointment wasn't my own error.

The attempts of us kids to retrieve fragments were little more than efforts to rebuild a castle with straw. We had failed to remember correctly; of course our failure was guaranteed because Mr. Watts hadn't given us the full story the first time around. I was surprised to discover the character of Orlick. In Mr. Dickens' version, Orlick is competing with Pip for Joe Gargery's favors. Ultimately Orlick will attack Pip's sister and leave her an insensible mess, a speechless invalid. He even tries to kill Pip! Why hadn't Mr. Watts told us this?

Also, it turns out there are two convicts on the marshes at the moment that Magwitch surprises Pip in the graveyard. Why hadn't Mr. Watts told us about the other convict? When Compeyson first turned up on the page I did not believe in him. I read on and discovered him to be a sworn enemy of Magwitch's. Compeyson turns out to be the same man who disappointed Miss Havisham on her wedding day. Years later, it is Compeyson who turns in Magwitch as he and Pip and Herbert Pocket sit mid-river in a boat, waiting for a steamship to spirit Magwitch out of England. Here, the pattern is clear. Pip is cast in his old role of savior. Only this time it is not to be.

In Mr. Dickens' version, as Compeyson directs a boat of militia towards them, Magwitch launches himself at his old adversary. The enemies tumble into the river. There is a struggle underwater from which Magwitch emerges the victor—a doomed victor while Compeyson drifts out of the story on the tide.

I suppose Miss Havisham's honor is upheld by Magwitch's vanquishing of Compeyson, but at what cost? Lives have been ruined all over the place.

At first, Mr. Watts' omissions made me angry. Why hadn't he stuck with Mr. Dickens' version? What was he protecting us from?

Possibly himself, or a rebuke from my mum, which I suppose adds up to the same thing. During the devil versus Pip debate the problem of finding the appropriate language had come up. Mr. Watts, ever conciliatory, tried to help her with the suggestion that people's imaginations sometimes got in the way. My mum, forever seeking advantage, countered by saying she thought it was a problem with blimmin' Dickens too.

On this occasion she had stayed on to listen to Mr. Watts read, and was able to retrieve a sentence from *Great*

Expectations that irritated her beyond all reason. *As I had grown accustomed to my expectations, I had insensibly begun to notice their effect upon myself and those around me.* Us kids sat back in our usual state of tremulous excitement reserved for these debates between my mum and Mr. Watts. We didn't see anything wrong with the sentence. Why, you could look out the open window and see that a statement about self-fulfillment was hardly a surprise to the grass or the flowers or the creepers growing everywhere.

My mum said she had no problem with stating the obvious. The problem was that silly blimmin' word *insensibly*. What was the point of that word? It just confused. If it hadn't been for that silly bloody *insensibly,* she'd have gotten it the first time. Instead, *insensibly* had led her to suspect it wasn't so straightforward after all.

She made Mr. Watts read the offending sentence and suddenly all of us kids saw what she was talking about. Maybe Mr. Watts as well. She said it was just "fancy nancy English talk." It's what you did to spice up a bland dish or to make a white dress more interesting by sewing in a red or blue hemline; that's what that word *insensibly* was there for—to pretty up a plain sentence. She thought Mr. Watts should remove the offending word.

At first, he said he couldn't; you couldn't muck around with Dickens. The word belonged to him; the whole sentence did. To whip out an inconvenient word would be an act of vandalism, like smashing the window of a chapel.

He said all that and I think from that day on he did the opposite. He pulled the embroidery out of Mr. Dickens' story to make it easier on our young ears.

Mr. Dickens. It took me a long time to drop the *Mister*. Mr. Watts, however, has remained Mr. Watts.

During those years in Townsville I went on reading Dickens with mixed enjoyment. I read *Oliver Twist, David Copperfield, Nicholas Nickleby, The Old Curiosity Shop, A Tale of Two Cities, Bleak House.* The book I kept coming back to was *Great Expectations*. I never tired of it. And with each rereading I got more out of it. Of course, for me it contains so many personal touchstones. To this day I cannot read Pip's confession—*It is a most miserable thing to feel ashamed of home*—without feeling the same of my island.

We are deep into the book, chapter 18 to be precise, when Pip discovers there is no going back to his old life on the marshes. For me, in my life, the same discovery had come much earlier. I was still a frightened black kid suffering from shock trauma when I'd looked down at the green of Honiara from the airplane, but I'd also known from that moment on there would be no return.

My mum belonged to all that I was trying to forget. I didn't want to forget her. But there was always a chance the other things would ride back on that memory. I'd see those soldiers again, smell my mum's fear as if she were standing right by me, here at the bus stop or in the library.

Sometimes I couldn't help it. I couldn't keep the door closed on that little room in my head where I'd put her. My mum kept her own hours and she could surprise me at any time of her own choosing. She would open that door and slap her hands down on her hips as if to ask, "Just what in the name of the Good Lord do you think you're up to?" I had stopped at the cosmetics counter. That's all. Or my eye caught up with the condoms sitting behind glass near the checkout operator. Those things belonged to a world that didn't include me yet, but I was beginning to think they could—at some time in the future.

Other times my mum popped up when you might expect her to. On one occasion, it was the sight of a mum with her daughter in the underwear department. The mum was as happy as a pig in molasses. She picked up one bra after another and waved it under the scornful eye of her daughter. The daughter locked herself away behind her folded arms. She refused to come out and play this game with her mum. Those arms were folded against any possibility of a mother's counsel breaking through to her.

I did not know that girl or her mum. But I knew the tension between them. It was unspoken and yet as powerful as the spoken word; it was invisible and yet as solid as a wall.

I stood there staring until a stroller banged into the backs of my legs. A small white boy shrieked at me. "Sorry," the mother said.

This is how I moved in the world of mothers and their kids, as a spectator wanders in a zoo, fascinated and repelled.

*

IN TOWNSVILLE, I won the senior English Prize. I walked across the stage to receive my certificate, and when I turned to face the applause I saw my father on his feet with his hands raised. He was so ridiculously proud of me. I was his champ. That's what he liked to call me. *Champ*. When we had visitors over he liked to wheel me out so he could say to them, "Ask her anything at all about Charles Dickens."

He was so proud of me. I didn't have the heart to tell him about Mr. Watts. I let him think I was all his own work.

I graduated from the University of Queensland. In my second year, at the start of the third semester, he flew down to Brisbane to visit. I met him at the airport and was surprised to see with him the woman who cleaned the house once a week. Her name was Maria. She was from the Philippines and her English wasn't very good. Now I saw her walk across the tarmac on my father's arm. His forehead was beaded with sweat. When I saw how nervous he was I felt childishly reassured. He still loved his Matilda.

Still, it wasn't the same after Maria moved in. She tried her best. In some ways she tried too hard. She wanted me to like her. But I couldn't love her like my mum. She asked me to talk about my mum. She said my father would not speak of her. I enjoyed hearing that.

My mum was a memory that could not be shared around, and besides, mention of her tended to shift our thoughts back to the island, and that wasn't a place either I or my dad wished to visit. Maria knew she couldn't replace my mum, but when she asked me to describe her I could only say, "She was a very brave woman, the bravest, and—just about everything about my dad made her angry." Maria laughed, and I smiled because I was off the hook.

⁂

PEOPLE SOMETIMES ASK ME "Why Dickens?," which I always take to be a gentle rebuke. I point to the one book that supplied me with another world at a time when it was desperately needed. It gave me a friend in Pip. It taught me you can slip under the skin of another just as easily as your own, even when that skin is white and belongs to a boy alive in Dickens' England. Now, if that isn't an act of magic I don't know what is.

Personally, though, I am loath to push *Great Expectations* onto anyone, my father especially. I am mindful of Mr. Watts' disappointment in Grace's inability to love what he loved, and I have never wanted to know that disappointment, or for my father to feel, as Grace must have, like a pup with a saucer of milk pushed towards her in the shape of a book. No. Some areas of life are not meant to overlap.

In Brisbane, for a time, I was a relief teacher in a big Catholic high school for boys. I learned that every teacher has a get-out-of-jail card. Mine was to read *Great Expectations* aloud. I would ask my new class to be quiet for ten minutes. That's all I asked for. If at the end of ten minutes they were bored, then they were free to get up and leave. They loved the idea of that. Mutiny rushed through their veins. Their faces grew bold with thoughts of what they would do.

Concealing my own smile, I would start at chapter one, the scene where the convict seizes Pip by the chin. *Show us where you live. Pint out the place*. You cannot read Dickens without putting in a little more effort. You cannot eat a ripe pawpaw without its innards and juice spilling down your chin. Likewise, the language of Dickens makes your mouth do strange things, and when you're not used to his words your jaw will creak. Anyway, I had to remember to stop after ten minutes. I'd look up and wait. No one ever rose from their desks.

Yet by the time I began my thesis on Dickens' orphans I knew more about a man I'd never met, except through his books and biographies, than I did of the man who had made the introduction.

I thank God for Maria coming along when she did because now I had an excuse not to return to Townsville. Maria and my dad needed some breathing space. But whenever I thought of them lying beneath the slow-moving bedroom fan, I got rid of Maria and stuck my mum there. I put my dad's arm around her shoulder. I stuck my mum's face on his chest. I stuck that smile on her that I'd seen in that photograph of my young parents in happier times.

I heard the relief in my dad's voice when I phoned to say I wouldn't be returning home at the end of the semester. I let him think I would be working over the summer break; I didn't tell him about a visit to Mr. Watts' old life in Wellington, New Zealand.

IT WAS DECEMBER. SO I DID NOT EXPECT TO find such a cold and drafty place. A wind hurled itself at trees, at people. Paper—I have never seen so much wind-blown paper—blew across the tarmac; it stuck in the overhead pylons. The seabirds kept out of the air and instead milled about in a school playground that I passed in a taxi.

I thought about Grace, fresh out of school, her face stuck to the window of a taxi such as the one that took me into the center of the small, bustling city. I stayed at a rowdy backpackers'. There were young people from every country. They had come here to climb, hike, surf, ski, bungee, to get drunk.

Much of what Mr. Watts had told us kids about his world came flooding back. The shock of brick in every direction. And the grass. Mr. Watts was right. Grass has far too much say. It fills windows. It lines streets. It marches away to hilltop after hilltop.

If Mr. Watts had held back certain characters from *Great Expectations,* who had he omitted from his own life?

I looked in the phone book. It had listings for forty-three Wattses. I can't remember if it was call number nine or number ten who said, "Oh, I think you want June Watts..." She named a street, and I found a J. Watts at that address. And when I dialed, the voice at the other end said, "Hello, June Watts speaking..."

"Is there a Mr. Watts?"

There was a pause. "Who is speaking?"

"My name is Matilda, Mrs. Watts. Your husband was my teacher..."

"Tom was?" I thought she was about to laugh, and then there was a different noise from her, as if maybe it was no surprise after all.

"This was a long time ago. On an island."

"Oh," she said. In the silence that followed I had a sense of her gathering herself. "So I take it you know that woman, Grace."

"Yes, Mrs. Watts," I said. "I knew of her. I did not really know her. Grace died some years back."

Nothing came from Mrs. Watts' end.

"I thought I might visit, Mrs. Watts," I said.

The silence lengthened into judgment.

"I was hoping..."

"I'm a bit tied up today," she said. "What did you say this is about?"

"Your husband, Mrs. Watts. He was my teacher."

"Yes. You said. But today is difficult. I was about to go out."

"I can only visit today. I fly back to Australia tomorrow afternoon."

There was an intake of breath. I waited with my eyes closed.

"Well, I suppose," she said. "It won't take long, will it?"

She gave me directions to her house, which involved catching a train. From the station there was a ten-minute walk through a neighborhood of brick houses, each with a bit of fenced land, and block walls; some were covered with bad words my mum would have taken a scrubbing brush to. Or else she would have stared those words down until they curled up with shame and dropped off the wall in flakes. I passed a sports field where I saw some bird life—ducks, magpies, seagulls—and a gang in hoods, their bums hanging out of baggy trousers, cuffs lapping over sneakers. And when I left the park behind I walked past a number of cold, wind-bashed houses with dried-up gardens.

June Watts had given me clear instructions. I was not to confuse A with B. Visitors to A would be met by a vicious dog.

This large, slow-moving woman in white slacks was not who I would have expected for Mr. Watts' wife. I did not think a wife of Mr. Watts' would wear a word on her top. It said "Smile." And thinking this might be a general expectation of hers, I did. She did not smile back.

I suppose I also came as a bit of a surprise. I imagine her expectations were based on the accent she heard on the phone, which was now distinctly Australian. I am sure she wasn't expecting someone this black. I wore black shoes too. And my black hair had grown out like it had during the blockade when my mum would threaten to pick me up and use my mop to scratch an itch on her back that she couldn't get to.

June Watts closed the door after me and showed me into a front room. Lace curtains guarded the windows and produced a sickly light. When without any warning Mrs. Watts clapped her hands, I jumped. A big gray cat resentfully got down from an armchair. Mrs. Watts directed me to the chair while she sat on the couch on the other side of the coffee table. There was a packet of cigarettes on the table. She reached for them and at the same moment tipped her eyes up at me. "You don't mind if I smoke?" she said. "I'm feeling nervous for some reason."

"Oh, there's no need to feel nervous of me, Mrs. Watts." I laughed to show how friendly I was. "I am very pleased you invited me here today. Your husband had a big influence on me."

"Tom did?"

She grunted like she had on the phone. She lit a cigarette and got up to open a window.

"I married a weak man, Matilda," she said. "I don't want to sound unkind, but it's true. Tom was not a brave man. He should have left me rather than carry on the way he did."

Mrs. Watts drew on her cigarette and exhaled. She waved the smoke away and returned to the couch.

"I don't suppose he told you any of that, did he?"

"I'm sorry, Mrs. Watts. Any of what, exactly?"

She turned her head to the hall.

"The other woman lived next door. That's A with the dog I told you about. I should have known something was going on. I used to catch him with his ear to the wall. I'd say, 'Tom, what on earth are you doing?' I can't remember what lie he told, there were so many, but he got away with it, didn't he, because not once did I suspect anything going on between those two. Even when she was taken off to Porirua and he used to go and visit, I had no reason to suspect."

"Porirua?"

"The mental hospital. You know, the loony bin." She paused to stub her cigarette out. "I can make a cup of tea if you'd like one."

"Thank you, Mrs. Watts. I would," I said.

There were photographs on the main wall. I tried to take them all in with a single glance. I did not want June Watts to think I was nosy. I *was* nosy, but I didn't want her to know. So I only remember one photo—of a young couple. He has dark hair and a lively face. His mouth is open with pink and white laughter. He wears a red flower in his buttonhole. She looks young, but her face is cold, not quite angry but prepared to be—in a pale blue dress and matching shoes. While June Watts fussed about in the kitchen I stared at the flower in the lapel of Mr. Watts' jacket. If we ran out of talk I thought I would ask after the name of that flower.

I joined her in the kitchen. She moved slowly. Her hip seemed to be the problem.

"Mrs. Watts, do you ever recall Mr. Watts wearing a red clown's nose?"

She dropped a tea bag into a cup and stopped to think.

"I never saw him with one on. Though it wouldn't surprise me." I waited for her to ask me why I had asked that question.

I went on waiting. If I were a dog I would have sat on my hindquarters and hung my tongue out. But she did not ask the question. She unplugged the jug and filled our cups. "I have some biscuits. Afghans."

"That would be nice, Mrs. Watts."

She said, "I don't have many visitors. I went out and got the afghans especially."

"Thank you, Mrs. Watts. That was very thoughtful."

I followed her back to the front room with the tray.

"I met Tom at the Standards Association. That's where we both worked. We were responsible for setting the standards for pretty much anything you can think of. The ratio of cement to water in all things. We were young. Everyone was young in those days. That's the main complaint you hear from people who are getting old. You stop seeing young people. You begin to wonder if there are any left and whether there were only young people when you were young."

I waited until she bit into her afghan before I did the same. Catching the crumbs in her hand, she said, "I didn't think about Grace much. I didn't give her nearly enough thought. She was always laughing." Mrs. Watts pulled a face. *Always laughing*. I understood this was a criticism. "It was like being around someone who is permanently pissed."

She reached for another cigarette and struck a match.

Her smoker's face concentrated. "So, how is Tom? The silly old bugger. It's been so long. Have you seen him recently?"

The cat clawing at the armchair caught her attention so she did not have any sense of my reeling backwards. I quickly composed myself and made a decision. "He was fine when I last saw him," I said. "But that was some years ago, Mrs. Watts. I live in Brisbane now."

"Well, I'm over it all now. It's all water under the bridge, isn't it? I have my own problems."

She paused, and I suppose it was for me to ask what those problems might be, but I was not interested. Instead I asked her what Mr. Watts had done at the Standards Association.

"Same as the rest of us," she said. "Clerical work and what have you. I was a secretary. Tom was in publications."

Then, perhaps it was because I did not know what to say to this woman that I thought to ask her, "Do you know what a mayfly is, Mrs. Watts?"

She gave me a puzzled look and I thought I would explain.

"The female larvae lie in mud at the bottom of a river for three years. Then they transform into winged insects, and as they fly from the water into the air they are impregnated by the waiting males."

Mrs. Watts' puzzled look turned into a frown.

"It is a story your husband told us kids."

"Tom did, did he? Well, Tom told lots of stories." She glanced at the plate between us. "Here, have another afghan. There's plenty more where that lot came from."

I knew that as soon as I left, Mrs. Watts would invite that big gray cat back into the room and the two of them would sit and watch television. That was one thing I had to get used to after I was reunited with my dad. The television. He hooted at it. He pointed at it. He got cross with it. He and the television laughed with one another as I tried to sleep in the next room. I did not say anything, because I understood that the television and my dad were close friends.

I looked over at the lace curtains. I could not imagine a young scholarship girl from the island living next door alone, and in a room like this. I looked out at the world. It was so silent out there. Mr. Watts once told us kids that silence was the first language he was born to. In a playful mood he told us how he'd stood on a rubbish bin and smashed its sides with a broom handle for something to do. He was five years old, and nothing resulted from his attack on the bin. Silence returned to fill the gaps in the shattered world. I understood there were no parrots where Mr. Watts was from. There was no wild shrieking that at the most unexpected moment can tear open your heart. There was just all this empty life where lantern blossom hung waiting to be admired and dogs prowled the street in search of an audience.

Sitting in the dead air of Mrs. Watts' living room, I thought, Grace must have seen that sky and those same slow-moving clouds. She must have had this same deathly drag on her heart that I felt.

I got up to leave.

"I suppose you know about his theater thing," Mrs. Watts said quickly.

I suspect it was her trump card. She wanted me to stay.

She crouched down on that bad hip of hers to ferret in a low bookcase until she yanked a scrapbook free. She slapped the dust off it and handed it to me. The scrapbook was filled with theater programs, reviews, and photographs of Mr. Watts playing various characters. I looked over the program covers—*An Inspector Calls, Pygmalion, The Odd Couple, Death of a Salesman*. These are just the ones I remember. There were so many of them, and so many photographs of Mr. Watts in costume. It was clear these productions were by an amateur theater group—there was the raised hand clasping the dagger, the flourishes of cape, and the insane glint in the eye of the jealous, the tormented, the dangerous, the vengeful—all those cheap and easy emotions that amateur theater is drawn to. I kept turning the pages.

"That's Tom in *The Queen of Sheba,*" June Watts said. "And that's her there. Queen bloody Sheba. The director had some funny ideas about that script." At that moment our eyes fell upon the same detail. "Oh look. You were asking about that. I remember now. The director thought Tom should wear a red clown's nose and the Queen of Sheba should stand in a trolley pulled by Tom to show some meeting of minds had been achieved. Don't ask me how or why..."

Mr. Watts and Grace looked so young. Without the help of June Watts I wouldn't have recognized them. But what was strange was Grace. She was smiling. I had never before seen her smile.

I must have been taking too long with the scrapbook because Mrs. Watts suggested I take it. When she saw me hesitate, she said, "It means nothing to me."

"Are you sure?"

"Well, what am I going to do with it?"

"It's very kind of you," I said.

She shrugged.

"It's just sitting there. And there's just me and Mr. Sparks here."

She meant the cat.

She saw me glance at my watch. "You have to go. All right," she said, and she painfully picked herself up off the floor.

As we stood at the door to say our good-byes she said, "My husband was a fantasist. I didn't know this when I married him."

"Mrs. Watts, can you tell me what happened to Grace? Do you know why she was taken to the mental hospital?"

"Queen of Sheba. She couldn't snap out of it," she said. "Couldn't. Wouldn't. Take your pick."

She frowned out at the street.

"Watch yourself. They'll skin you for your clothes."

I looked out at the same stark street but didn't see another soul.

I thanked her for the afghans and the scrapbook. I was in a hurry to get back to town but realized I had one last question.

"Mrs. Watts, is there someone by the name of Miss Ryan?"

"Eileen Ryan. Why yes. She used to live at the end of the street." She turned to point out the house, then seemed to catch herself. "Why do you ask?"

I ignored the question. "Does she have a big rambling garden?"

"She did years ago. Yes. But she's dead now. She was blind, you know. Eileen Ryan." She looked at me. "How do you know that name? Tom used to mow her lawns for her."

*

I HAD A FRAGMENT. The acting part of Mr. Watts. So, what about it? The fact he enjoyed acting gnaws away with its questions of sincerity. Especially when I think about Mr. Watts' classroom gestures. The stare to the back of the room. His eyes rolling up to the ceiling. The studied pose of a man thinking and considering.Was this Mr. Watts, or an actor playing Mr. Watts the schoolteacher? Who was it that us kids saw in the classroom? A man who genuinely thought *Great Expectations* to be the greatest novel by the greatest English writer in the nineteenth century? Or a man left with only a morsel who will claim it the best meal of his life?

I suppose it is possible to be all of these things. To sort of fall out of who you are into another, as well as to journey back to some essential sense of self. We only see what we see. I have no idea of the man June Watts knew. I only know the man who took us kids by the hand and taught us how to reimagine the world, and to see the possibility of change, to welcome it into our lives. Your ship could come in at any time, and that ship could take many forms. Your Mr. Jaggers might even turn out to be a log.

I had hoped to get more from my visit to Mrs. Watts. I guess I was hoping to have heard stories. I had the scrapbook, and it answered the mystery about the red nose. Otherwise, Mr. Watts was as elusive as ever. He was whatever he needed to be, what we asked him to be. Perhaps there are lives like that—they pour into whatever space we have made ready for them to fill. We needed a teacher, Mr. Watts became that teacher. We needed a magician to conjure up other worlds, and Mr. Watts had become that magician. When we needed a savior, Mr. Watts had filled that role. When the redskins required a life, Mr. Watts had given himself.

MR. DICKENS WAS EASIER TO UNDERSTAND than Mr. Watts. For one thing, more of his life is available and on show. Shelves of libraries are given over to the life of Dickens and his works. An interest in Dickens is more easily rewarded than any effort at playing Mr. Detective and investigating the life of Mr. Watts. The contents of Dickens' life have been ransacked and sifted over by experts, and I was well on my way to becoming one of them.

For a long time all I knew about this dead man was what Mr. Watts told us kids, and what I could glean from a sneaked look at the back cover of Mr. Watts' copy of *Great Expectations.* Mr. Dickens looked exactly how I would have wanted him to look. I was reassured by his beard. It wasn't tidy, but as with Mr. Watts' own beachcomber's variety it did look inevitable and therefore right. I also liked his narrow frame contained by a waistcoat. I had an idea he would be kind. His crinkly, warm eyes supported that idea. And so do his many articles on the poor and orphaned, which I pored over in the British Library on Euston Road in London.

Spread before me were all the fragments of life that had gone into the making of *Great Expectations*. I could magpie through all his personal papers. I could study his own handwriting. I could look at the same things he had looked at—the stone-cold streets, the soaring ambition of the buildings, the vagrants, the drunks, the muddy banks of lives stuck and in decline—and trace the view back to the imagined one.

At first, hardly a day passed when I did not congratulate myself on landing here in Mr. Dickens' city. I also loved the sweet feeling of privilege, which never failed me, as I presented my ID card to a bored guard in black uniform sitting behind a clear desktop.

You enter a room lined with long desks, and lamplight that is not too bright or too dim, but just right. Everything was just right. I loved the fact you could call up anything—in my case, papers, books, and articles on and by Dickens himself—and within the hour that material would be found in the bowels of this great library. For the first few months of this I felt blessed.

There were, however, times when I wished I had someone to share what I had found. That Dickens, like Mr. Watts, was not quite the man I thought he was. The man who writes so touchingly and powerfully about orphans cannot wait to turn his own kin out the door. He wants them out in the world. He worries that home will smother their ambition. He wants them carving their own way by dint of hard work.

So his son Walter is packed off to India before he is seventeen and dies aged twenty-two. Sydney dies in the navy in his twenties. Francis joins the Bengal Mounted Police, but affected by a stammer he flees to the wilderness and dies in Canada aged forty-two.

Alfred and Plorn, Dickens dispatches to Australia. Edward's his favorite, "his darling Plorn." "I need not tell you that I love you dearly and am very, very sorry in my heart to part with you. But this life is half made up of partings, and these pains must be borne." Australia, his father decides, will sort him out and flush out his natural abilities.

*

ONE MORNING I delayed my daily trip to the British Library to visit the old Foundling Hospital in Brunswick Square. These days it is an orphans museum. It is very grand. You mount a wide sweep of steps. Inside, its walls are covered with painterly scenes of the orphanage; in some, the mothers line up to hand their babies over. I remember my own mum holding her arms out to me. I remember the slow open and close of her airless mouth. I remember feeling torn apart. Yet on the faces of the mums in the paintings I could find no trace of distress. You see the same slightly bored faces at a supermarket checkout. How easy it is, these paintings report, to hand over your child. In the gallery upstairs I found a more accurate picture in the form of glass cabinets filled with buttons, acorns, hairclips, pennies with holes drilled—tiny, pathetic keepsakes mums left behind for their babies to remember them by. A pointless exercise, it turns out, because the first thing the orphanage did was to change the baby's name. With a different name their old history would end and a new one would begin. Pip could become Handel.

*

GRAVESEND IS WHERE I would have ended *Great Expectations*. Gravesend. And this is where I came one cold day in late May. I walked past benches filled with silent Indian men in colorful turbans, a layer of sadness dampening their cheeks. I saw them sneak a look at me, a young woman blacker than any they had ever seen. I saw their eyes and their wonder. What is she thinking? That black girl with the darting white eyes. What does she know about this landscape?

I could tell them the landscape from *Great Expectations* is gone, that its fabled marshes lie beneath motorways and industrial estates. I could tell them that the story has new custodians. These custodians were once a bunch of black kids, who I believe still wake in the early hours to remember another time, when they drifted between an island and a blacksmith's, on the marshes in England in eighteen-hundred-and-something.

You have to work a bit harder in Dickens' old neighborhood to see what he did. The emigrant ships are ghosts.

The sight of bareheaded men and women waving handkerchiefs from the decks are history, bones in some cemetery on the other side of the world.

There is a nicely paved river walk, and if you walk in the same direction taken by the old emigrant ships, it is impossible not to think about departure. Leave. Go. Get away. Make yourself new.

There is the river, pointing the way out of this muddy world. As I wandered past the mission, where emigrants were rowed ashore to say a few prayers as insurance for their sea journey into the unknown, I found myself thinking back to the last time I was alone with Mr. Watts.

I had not thought about that conversation for years. Like so many things, I probably blocked it out. I wonder now, at that moment he turned away, if Mr. Watts had made up his mind to leave the island without me. Because it seems to me, thinking about it all these years later, that what I felt was a parting, a line drawn. I have called it a line, but maybe it is better to talk about a curtain. A curtain dropped between Mr. Watts and his most adoring audience. He would move on and I would shift into that burial ground occupied by figures of the past. I would be a small speck on a large island as he sat in Mr. Masoi's boat motoring from one life to another. I knew that is what would happen, would have happened, because it had happened to me. The moment I left I never looked back.

*

THERE WAS THE LONG TRAIN ride back to London Bridge. I felt inexplicably downhearted. As if I had fallen backwards into myself. And I was back with mourning before that flood erased everything. I looked out the carriage window. The baby green leaves of spring growth made no impression on my glum mood. The singing conductor failed to win a smile from me.

When I left the station I had to drag myself up the steps to street level. This tiredness. Where had it come from? I knew what it was to climb steep tracks in the hills. What were a few flights of filthy steps lined with beggars and Gypsy kids whose eyes moved faster than any fish I ever saw?

I walked home wishing I had some other place to go. I climbed the stale carpet of the stairs in the boardinghouse and, opening the door to my bedsit, stood for a moment on the threshold, unable to enter.

There were the trappings of my life—the mounted photograph of Dickens, an article blown up to poster size announcing publication of *Great Expectations* in book form. There was my desk and that pile of paper known as my thesis. It had sat there all day waiting for me to get back from Gravesend with fresh material. It had sat there like Mr. Watts had once, with his secret exercise book, waiting for fragments. Well, I didn't have any fresh material. All I had lugged back with me was this heaviness, which sat deep inside, in my bones, and which had come over me quickly like bad weather.

The only thing I could think to do was to get into bed. And there I stayed.

For six days I didn't get up except to make a cup of tea, or fry an egg, or lie in the skinny bath gazing at a cracked ceiling. The days punished me with their slowness, piling up the hours on me, spreading their joylessness about the room.

I listened to the buses change down gear outside the boardinghouse. I listened to the hiss of tires on the wet road. I lay in bed listening to the woman downstairs get ready for work. I listened to her run the shower and the shrill whistle on her kettle. I waited for her footsteps on the path below my window, and as that brief contact with the world departed I shut my eyes and begged the walls to let me go back to sleep.

A doctor would have said I was suffering from depression. Everything I have read since suggests this was the case. But when you are in the grip of something like that it doesn't usefully announce itself. No. What happens is you sit in a dark, dark cave, and you wait. If you are lucky there is a pinprick of light, and if you are especially lucky that pinprick will grow larger and larger, until one day the cave appears to slip behind, and just like that you find yourself in daylight and free. This is how it happened for me.

⁂

ONE MORNING I woke and threw back the covers. I was up before the woman downstairs. I walked across to my desk. I was being urged to do something I had put aside for too long. I took the top sheet of paper from "Dickens' Orphans," turned it over, and wrote "Everyone called him Pop Eye."

I wrote that sentence six months ago. Everything that follows I wrote over the intervening months. I have tried to describe the events as they happened to me and my mum on the island. I have not tried to embellish. Everyone says the same thing of Dickens. They love his characters. Well, something has changed in me. As I have grown older I have fallen out of love with his characters. They are too loud; they are grotesques. But strip away their masks and you find what their creator understood about the human soul and all its suffering and vanity. When I told my father of my mum's death he broke down and wept. That is when I learned there is a place for embellishment after all. But it belongs to life—not to literature.

⁂

I HAD DECIDED to leave England, but had one more farewell task to perform. This involved a visit to Rochester, where Dickens pinched one or two landmarks for *Great Expectations.*

In Rochester you arrive at a place you know you feel obliged to like. There it is—the perfect postcard of how an English village is supposed to have looked like in eighteen-hundred-and-something. You trip over the cobbles and choke on the sentimentality. Everywhere you look Dickens is a shopkeeper, a restaurateur, a merchant in secondhand goods. You find you have the choice between Fagin's Café or eating at Mrs. Brumbles or A Taste of Two Cities.

I called myself Pip, and came to be called Pip is one of the most endearing lines in literature. This is who I am: please accept me as you find me. This is what an orphanage sends its charges out to the world with. This is what emigrants wash up on Pacific shorelines with. This is what Mr. Watts had asked the rambos to accept. But I could not accept a blimmin' fruit and veg shop named after Pip as in Pip's of Rochester.

There were another two hours to fill before I caught the train back to London, so I decided to tag on to the end of a guided tour. A woman from the Charles Dickens Center at Eastgate House led the party up the stairs of the town hall into a long room where Pip was signed over into an apprenticeship with Joe Gargery.

From the town hall there was a short walk up the hill, and at some point I realized that we were taking the same route as Pip had on his way to visit Miss Havisham. The same route which was known to me, having walked it before as a besotted reader on an island on the other side of the world.

The woman from the center pointed out a two-story manor—this was Satis House. Here I learned something new. Mr. Dickens pinched the name and stuck it on a larger and more imposing mansion next to the brewery, where he installed Miss Havisham and Estella.

After a short walk through a park, we stood across the

road, staring back at the gates, the same gates where Estella first receives Pip and condescends to call him "boy." A taxi drew up and a yuppyish young man bounced out. He gave us a quick glance. I thought he looked annoyed. The guide said Miss Havisham's house had been turned into apartments.

We watched the young man let himself in the gate and walk up the path. We watched him set his briefcase down and put a key in the door. The door opened and closed. After that we let our eyes drift. We stood there for some time drifting with our eyes and thoughts. "Well," someone said at last.

The tour ended back at Eastgate House. I followed the others up the stairs, and there I encountered Miss Havisham in her white wedding gown. She was stuck behind glass, her back turned to us sightseers. There for all eternity. I wished she could turn, just for half an instant, to find a black woman staring at her.

The tour ended in Mr. Dickens' study. A mannequin of the author himself reclined in a leather chair, his legs sprawled before him, his hands in gentle repose. His sleepy eyelids at half-mast. We had walked in on Mr. Dickens while he was daydreaming. Behind the restraining rope, the man standing next to me heard me whisper, "I have met Mr. Dickens and this is not him." He smiled and looked away. I did not try and convince him. But if I had, this is what I would have said.

The Mr. Dickens I had known also had a beard and a

lean face and eyes that wanted to leap from his face. But my Mr. Dickens used to go about barefoot and in a buttonless shirt. Apart from special occasions, such as when he taught, and then he wore a suit.

It has occurred to me only recently that I never once saw him with a machete—his survival weapon was story. And once, a long time ago and during very difficult circumstances, my Mr. Dickens had taught every one of us kids that our voice was special, and we should remember this whenever we used it, and remember that whatever else happened to us in our lives our voice could never be taken away from us.

For a brief time I had made the mistake of forgetting that lesson.

In the worshipful silence I smiled at what else they didn't know. Pip was my story, even if I was once a girl, and my face black as the shining night. Pip is my story, and in the next day I would try where Pip had failed. I would try to return home.

Acknowledgments

I want to thank Michael Heyward and Melanie Ostell of Text for the wonderful confidence and enthusiasm they showed in *Mister Pip* from the first day it arrived as a manuscript. To Melanie, for her astute editorial probing and suggestions; to Michael, for guiding the book out into the world.

And I especially want to thank my longtime publisher, Geoff Walker of Penguin Books New Zealand, and my agent, Michael Gifkins, for their unflagging efforts on my behalf and *Mister Pip*'s.

A grant from Creative New Zealand helped toward the writing of this book, for which I remain extremely grateful.

About the Author

LLOYD JONES was born in New Zealand in 1955. His best-known works include *The Book of Fame,* winner of numerous literary awards, *Biografi,* a *New York Times* Notable Book, *Choo Woo, Here at the End of the World We Learn to Dance,* and *Paint Your Wife*. He lives in Wellington, New Zealand.